THE ORIGINAL MEERKAT
AND OTHER SHORTWEIRD STORIES

MARCEL ST. PIERRE

The Original Meerkat & Other Shortweird Stories

Paperback version ISBN 978-1-7778451-2-4

ISBN 978-1-7778451-3-1 (hardcover)

ISBN 978-1-7778451-4-8 (ebook)

Published by Shortweird Productions
Toronto, ON

www.shortweird.com

Cover design by Mike Butler of Cubbyhole Studios

The Original Meerkat

and other

Shortweird Stories

MARCEL ST. PIERRE

SHORTWEIRD PRESS

For everyone who made it through
the pandemic alive and in one piece,
but especially for those who did not.

Table Of Contents

Overachiever

Targle Grumjeel's parents had always gone to great lengths to instill in them a sense of self-esteem and a desire to pursue excellence in all things. "You can be anything you want to be," they said. "There is nothing you can't do. You can achieve anything."

Even a little encouragement goes a long way, and in the direct path of this positive nurturing, Targle did indeed prove to be exceptional in the field of unmatchable accomplishments.

While still in high-school, Targle broke the language barrier between man and dolphin. Their rogue startup company *Targle Motors* was famously founded on a dare, and soon invented a car that ran on lies. *Targle For Men* produced a line of beard oil so luxurious that one customer's goatee became sentient, shaved itself off the man's face while he was sleeping, and is now teaching string theory at MIT. And of course, who can forget when *The Targle Foundation Of The Un-Impossible* found Amelia Earhart? Never mind history's insistence that she'd died when her plane went down in the Pacific; within a year of setting their sights on the goal, the pilot was found both dead and alive, in every ocean in the world. Impossible, yes. Nonsensical? Of course. But true.

But a life lived oblivious to limitations is a double edged sword. Simply put, nobody ever told Targle they could fail. And that is why, now, while it's true Targle's record for highest Olympic ski jump is unlikely to ever be broken, Targle has also been in orbit for six years, and must be presumed dead.

Darby

The widow Jaundice Beezer had always employed fashionable lateness to make herself seem busy and important, because she was neither. And so it was that today, as always, Jaundice arrived at *Café Vedova* a full seventy-three minutes later than when she and her fellow widows Zarla and Jorma had agreed to meet.

After exchanging widow-ish pleasantries (Am I late? Oh, of course not! What a beautiful scarf! Is it new? Yes! Is it silk? Oh, I don't think so. It must be silk! Yes, I think you're right!) she sat down with them at their favourite table in front of their favourite storefront window. The tea menus arrived, and they settled into the routinely fussy business of living large by staying small.

As usual, Zarla threatened to try something new, maybe something with the word 'zinger' in the name. Jorma voiced her curiosity about jasmine; didn't it sound just a tiny bit exotic, and didn't they deserve a little excitement once in a while, having outlived their husbands?

But change and newness had always threatened Jaundice, so she reminded them, yet again, that the 'darjeeling' district was dangerously full of tigers, and should they be supporting that? And 'Earl Grey' sounded a bit slutty, didn't they agree, and really a perfectly sensible orange pekoe was probably the best choice to go with their tiny sandwiches and biscuits, wouldn't they say so? And as usual, that's just what they said, and Jorma sighed to herself in relief that yet again, at least for now, she was still busy, important, and terribly influential.

Just then, another older woman wearing large aviator goggles and flapping wings of torn fabrics and trash bags ran headlong into the street-facing window behind them with a shuddering thwonk. She bounced backwards through the air, tracing a magnificent arc before landing in a crumpled and shuddering heap on the sidewalk.

Zarla and Jorma flinched and clucked with concern, but Jaundice kept studying her menu, feigning nonchalance but secretly dripping with contempt and fear. "Well," she said finally, when she felt her voice wouldn't give away the feelings of worthlessness and unimportance bubbling up inside of her. "I see Darby still thinks she's a bird?"

The Séance

Well, I forget who suggested it, but in hindsight, I do declare, contacting the Rougarou was a terrible mistake. You heard of the Rougarou, ain't you? Don't feel bad if you ain't, it's a very specific kind of swampy, shapeshifty, cajun boogeyman dog thing from Louisiana, I guess, and tell you the truth, I never much heard of him before my Mardi-Gras themed séance last year.

I wanted us to contact Bloody Mary or Satan or something sensible like that, but I also wanted to be a good host and stick to the theme of the night, so fine, I say, Rougarou it is, whatever. Well, first red flag, he was only too easy to summon! I don't think the medium ever even finished asking for a sign of his presence when there's this big blast of brimstone and smoke, and there he is! Sitting cross legged in the middle of the table, if you please, half man, half dog or whatever, naked as a jaybird except for his parade beads and a crucifix hanging around his neck. He smiles that big toothy grin at us and goes "Who dat?" in this Rapides Parish accent that almost sounds fake. "I'm de fuckin' Rougarou!"

Then don't he just lean back to balance himself on his buttocks in a boat pose? Big ol' show-off. "'Tree-sixty 'ere we go," he says, and he opens his legs in a wide vee and spins around and puckers out a fart at each one of us at the table. Oh, and he's giving his own play by play, too! "Ungh! Dat's for you, cher! Ungh! Fais-do-do! Ungh! Étoufée! Ungh! Beaucoup! Don't say I never gave you nuttin'," etcetera, you get the picture, I ain't got to act it out. It was gross. One hundred percent no class.

Well, at this point I know them caterers are all set up in the dining room so I says let's break early, even though ain't nobody hungry now. I says to Rougarou thanks for coming, you know, sorta like a "don't let us keep you here all night" kinda thing? Well, not only don't he take the hint, he spends the rest of the soiree just being a pest!

We do our best to just keep ignoring him. I mean, we have moved on, honey, don't feed the troll, you know? But he's like "C'mon, I'm just try'n to pass a good time wit' y'all" and he's touching everybody's food with his dick when they ain't looking, or he's humping them to assert dominance, or he's cornering them in long, pointless conversations about crawdaddies and how them vaccines make you magnetic to spoons. He's even making people take selfies with him, and then he's poking fun at everyone 'cause, oh guess why? Oh, you can't catch that ol' Rougarou on no camera, oh, ha ha, ain't *you* stupid? I swear he even ate one of us! I mean, I can't prove he ate one of us but I didn't see Meredith leave and she ain't called me back in months. I just don't think that's a coincidence, do you?

Anyway, he was fit to be tied, let me tell you. An actual monster. And when I finally tells him to leave point blank? Well don't he turn out to be some drama queen!

"Oh, naw! Don't make me go back into dat ouija board, cher," he says, and then he goes prancing about the room, draping himself across every piece of furniture like some Victorian lady having the vapours, and he's tipping over vases, he's pulling books off the shelves, he throws the cat out the window. She's fine, she landed three balconies down, but me? I just had enough at that point. "Sir? Sir!" I tells him. "If I wasn't clear the first time, you are not welcome here no mo', no way, no how. Do you feel me?" Well, now, he does not like that one bit, and he just stares me down with them big yellow eyes, and I thought, oh, we is gonna have a scrap here tonight!

But naw, instead don't he just throw this big old tantrum? He sets to bawlin' and howlin' and he flips that séance table over, then he shoves that ouija planchette up his butt and gives us all the finger. "Never meet your heroes, bitches, yeah, you right!" he yells, and then, oh my God!

Not a word of lie, but then doesn't he start playing with himself? Right there in the middle of the room! And the whole time he's going "Crawdaddy, crawdaddy, I'm so close, lookit me! Don' lookit me! Lookit me! I'm de Rougarou! I'm de Rougarou..!" And only then does he start fading back into spirit form or whatever, but we can still hear him and it takes him like an hour to fade completely out of sight. Talk about are you done yet? Even now, over a year later, I can't have anyone in that games room because it still smells like Rougarou ass.

Anyway, I learnt my lesson, for sure. It was all a bit much, but that's why the price on my condo is so low. I am what you might call a motivated seller.

The Mayor

The Mayor could put out fires just by looking at them. On its own, this would be considered an amazing gift, a superpower of sorts. The relative merits of this singular ability were somewhat dampened, however, by the fact that the mayor also suffered from sleep-arson.

The affliction is exactly what it sounds like. Time after time, he'd fitfully get out of bed, still asleep, then walk or even drive himself to locations blocks or even miles from his home. There, he'd set fires using anything he found or brought to the scene; kerosene, old newspapers, Molotov cocktails, oily rags, a flamethrower and, in one case, static electricity from a balloon rubbed against a possum for three hours.

Over the years, the mayor's detractors voiced their full-throated umbrage over a growing body of photographic and video evidence - not to mention an exposé on 60 Minutes - that had captured the somnambulant Mayor setting these fires. His fervent supporters simply pointed to the plethora of times the mayor had put out all those fires the very next morning by simply affixing them with a stern gaze. "It's the least I could do," he'd say, and his supporters would get behind that as the reason that proved he was a great guy, after all. Almost like one of them, wasn't he?

Many political opponents railed for the town to start a fire brigade at the very least, but the mayor always won the vote against it. Hadn't he proven many times he himself could put out fires, just by looking at them? "Isn't this a redundancy and a waste of taxpayer dollars?" he'd ask, and his acolytes would froth at the mouth and fall over each other in fits of agreement. And this kind of common sense argument combined with keeping taxes low kept the majority of voters in love with him.

The tragic loss of heritage buildings and human life were never enough to convince anybody to run against him. It has been a conundrum and a source of local controversy, to say the least. And while nobody in town has gone so far as to say democracy is broken, it's a sore point in some circles that he's expected to win the next election, by acclamation, yet again next fall. But what can you do?

Wall Phone

I used to rent an apartment that had an old rotary wall phone, halfway down the hallway that led from the front entrance to the kitchen.

It was a dark bluish-black, or blackish-blue depending on what time of day it was and how the light was hitting it. The numbers on the wheel behind the finger holes were mostly worn away, so I figured this thing had been there since at least the early 1960s. There was never any dial tone if you picked up the receiver, and aside from the long coiled wire connecting the handset to the base there were no other wires or cables leading to or from it. It was really a bit of a useless artifact, but I kind of liked how it looked on the wall. It was a conversation starter, if you will, even if you couldn't use it to have a conversation any more. It added a touch of character to the place, so I did what I assume other tenants before me had done about it.

Nothing.

But then one morning as I was having breakfast that phone rang. Who could be calling my wall phone, I wondered, then reminded myself it wasn't <u>my</u> wall phone as much as it was a phone on my wall that I knew nothing about. Semantics aside, while picking up the receiver would be the polite thing to do, it also just felt very active and very much like something I shouldn't do if I wanted to mind my own business. Which I did. It rang maybe five or six times, and then it stopped.

Chalking it up to a random electromagnetic discharge or some other perfectly scientific explanation, I left for the day and didn't give it another thought. I'd completely forgotten about it when it rang again a few weeks later.

Same thing: five or six rings just as I was having breakfast, and then it was silent. I kept my promise with myself not to get involved. It was silent for another couple of weeks, and then it rang again around the same time. The only constant was my steadfast refusal to answer it. I was determined to live with it and ignore it.

This went on for at least three or four months, but then it began to ring every three or four days, and at any time of day, not just at breakfast.

Sometimes it rang at suppertime. Sometimes it rang in the evening. Sometimes it would even ring and wake me up well after midnight. It seemed this phone was bent on proving that it would not be ignored. This left me with more questions than answers.

How long indeed had this phone been there? Why was this happening? Was there a perfectly simple explanation? Did it ring when I was at work? I caught myself for the first time wondering if the caller knew when I was home, and the thought of there actually being a caller gave me shivers. Was there really somebody on the other end of the line? Did the caller know me? Was this some weird true-life episode of a dark anthology television series and I was about to find out I was both the caller and the recipient? I lost several nights of sleep after scaring myself with that last thought, but despite all my questions and fears, I still resolved never to answer the phone, because for sure it was none of my business.

A year went by. Then early one morning it happened to ring just as I was walking by it, and whether it was carelessness, drowsiness, stupidity or fate, I instinctively lifted the receiver to my ear without thinking. "Hello?" I said, only then realizing my knee-jerk misstep. I almost hung up, but instead I gasped and froze at the sound of someone breathing on the other end.

"Hello?" I said again, my whole body tingling with anticipation. There was a long pause.

"Hello…" said the caller, sounding as tentative and afraid as I was. I felt faint. I kept telling myself to hang up now, that this was none of my business, that I wanted to get off this ride, that I could stop what I'd set in motion right now, no harm, no foul, but try as I might, I could not put the handset back in its cradle.

"Yes?" I said, cursing myself for getting involved. "Who's calling?"

"Yeah… uh," they stammered, then paused. "Is, um… is this… could I speak to Alaglabeth?"

"Who?"

"Alaglabeth."

"Alaglabeth?"

"Yeah, is Alaglabeth there?"

"I'm sorry, Alaglabeth?"

"Yeah."

"You want to speak to someone named Alaglabeth?"

"Yeah."

"Well, who is this?" I asked.

"What?"

"Who is calling?"

"Who, me?"

"Yes. Are you the one who's been calling this number?"

"Yeah."

"Then who are you? It's rude to not identify yourself."

There was a long pause on the line, and then, very hesitantly, the caller replied. "This is an ear."

"What?"

"I'm an ear."

"An ear? You're an ear?"

"Yeah."

There was another awkward pause, and I tried to make a joke. "So this is like the expression, the walls have ears?"

"What?"

"I said this is like the expression, the walls have ears."

"I don't get it."

"Well, it's…er," I stammered. "Because this phone number you've been dialing has been ringing an old phone on my wall. So, if you're just an ear, then my wall .. has an ear? I guess … you know what I mean? "

"Oh, so like the wall have ears?" they replied.

"Sure."

"I get it now."

"Okay…"

"I never heard that expression before."

"It's pretty well known."

"I never heard it before."

"Really?"

"Yeah."

"So." There was another long pause. "So, you're really just an ear?" I asked again.

"Yeah."

"Okay. And you're the one who keeps calling this number?"

"Yeah. I guess so. Unless other people are calling, too?"

"No, nobody else is calling. And you're calling to speak to Alaglabeth?"

"Yeah."

"Why?"

"What?"

Ears may be good listeners, but this one sure didn't hear or communicate very well at all. Getting details was like pulling teeth with this one, but I managed to learn that Alaglabeth was some girl they'd met at a bar. She'd scribbled her name and this number on a napkin, stuck it in their lobe and they'd been trying to call her ever since.

I told them for sure there was nobody named Alaglabeth

living here.

I agreed it was a pretty common name, I supposed, but for sure I didn't know anybody named Alaglabeth and no, I wasn't just her boyfriend or her brother or her roommate screening her calls.

The ear asked if I thought Alaglabeth had faked her number in the first place, and I'll be honest, for sure I think that's what happened. A hundred percent that's what happened. But they sounded like they were going to break down and cry so I said maybe she had just written it down wrong on account of being drunk or dyslexic or something, and that seemed to make the ear feel a little better.

I agreed for sure dating must be pretty tough for someone who is just an ear.

"I guess it just wasn't meant to be," they sighed. And then they were silent for a long time. "Are you still there?" they finally asked.

"Yeah," I replied. "I'm still here. So, was that it?"

"Yeah, I guess so," they said.

"Cool," I said. "Well. I'm gonna hang up now."

"Yeah. Okay," they said, lapsing into another long silence.

"Okay," I said.

"Okay."

"Okay."

"Okay, I guess."

And as rude as it seemed I finally did actually just hang up without saying goodbye, because, I mean, it was really none of my business.

The ear called another half dozen times over the next couple of weeks, and I kept picking up, surprising myself each time. Why did this ear keep calling? Didn't they know Alaglabeth didn't live here anymore, if she ever did? After a while I stopped picking up, but the phone just kept ringing. One night I almost took a crowbar to the phone, just to end it, but I didn't. Does violence ever solve anything? Instead, I put in a notice with my landlord and moved out the next month. Like I said before, it was really none of my business. I know they were just lonely and needed a friend, but I'm just one shoulder, and believe me I get tired of being cried on.

Truth or Dare

F liz was sleeping soundly as the first few rays of dawn trickled over the horizon, pooling up slowly at the small of her back, tickling her awake. She slowly woke and turned her head towards the warm golden light, grateful for warmth after the last few chilly hours, but her head was pounding. She groaned slightly and brought up one hand to shield her eyes.

She could hear the waves lapping on the shore.

She could hear the twittering of morning birds.

And she could hear the snore coming from the warm body she was spooning, marring the otherwise perfect tranquility of the moment with an apneatic squeal. Braft.

Fliz had hooked up with Braft the night before. They'd traded messages on a dating app for a few weeks, and she'd felt nothing but good vibes about him when they'd finally talked on the phone. She'd agreed to meet him at his place, just a few blocks north of the beach.

Braft had been even better in person than online; the perfect gentleman. He had been smart without mansplaining. He'd been engaging and present without being 'on' all the time. He listened when she was speaking. He was well read without being elitist, well-travelled but not a snob about it. He knew how to pair wine and he'd made an amazing dinner. His only flub, if she were being fussy and had to criticize anything, had been his overly flirtatious presentation of what he called his favourite dessert: sex on the beach.

"Well, that's a bit on the nose," she'd teased.

"Flattery will get you everywhere," he'd retorted.

But as lame as the suggestive dessert had been, it had been delicious. Braft had genuinely been charming as hell the whole evening. Maybe it was the wine. Or the tequila shots. Or that she hadn't had sex in a year. But in any case, after dessert, they each took another bottle of wine in hand and walked three blocks down to the woodsy beachfront of Edwards Lake.

He lit a bonfire, from whose flickering light they were soon cuddling beside. After a bit more drinking and a lot of making out, they playfully settled into a few rounds of "truth or dare". Fliz revealed many silly and semi-serious things about herself, but Braft always chose the dare. And she'd had a lot of dares for him.

The dares had escalated from kissing to rubbing to zipper play and pants-around-ankles nonsense till she finally insisted that he play 'truth' at least once. "I like dares better," he said, coyly. "But we can stop if you're feeling uncomfortable?"

Fliz had to admit she hadn't felt this comfortable with another person in a long time.

"Fine. I dare you…" she began, pausing as a delicious idea

formed in her head."Okay," she smiled, remembering something she hadn't done since she was a schoolgirl. "I dare you," she repeated, then giggled, her cheeks beginning to flush. "Forget it. Never mind, it's stupid…"

"What is it?" asked Brad.

"I mean the town council made it illegal…" she continued. "It was so bad for tourism."

"Now I'm really curious," said Braft.

"Alright," she said, leaning in and whispering hotly in his ear. "I dare you to let me hogtie you naked here on the beach, so you can be devoured at dawn as an offering to the Lake Edwards Monster."

"Uh-oh," Braft laughed. "Is it too late for me to pick 'truth' instead?"

"No. No, of course not," she said, doing her best to hide her disappointment. "It's a lot."

"Psyche!" said Braft as he stood up, ditching the rest of his clothes till he stood, naked and aroused in front of her. "Let's do this!"

With permission granted, Fliz hip-checked him to the ground. She pulled out the many feet of rope she always kept in her hair and hog-tied him then and there. He said nothing, and his complete submission made her so hot that, after checking the tightness of the knots, she took off the rest of her own clothes and they had the sort of rough, rope-burn, gritty-sandy sex-adjacent fun that you would (or wouldn't) expect under the circumstances. Spent and satisfied, she had finally fallen asleep in a heap beside his trussed and incapacitated body.

And now as she slowly woke up, she smiled to herself. She really liked him, she thought. Maybe the monster wouldn't eat this one? And with that thought, her eyes finally snapped open.

The monster.

She bolted upright, gasping. "Braft, wake up," she whispered hoarsely as she gathered and threw on her clothes. "We have to get up."

"Hmn?"

"Braft," she hissed under her breath, this time kicking him in the butt. "We have to go before the monster gets here! Get up!"

"Mph?" said Braft.

She fumbled urgently in the sand till she found his pants and threw them at him. "Here, put these on, quickly!"

"Mm, 'kay..." he said, rolling over as best he could, since he was still hogtied. "Oh my God! I forgot I tied you up!" she said as she began trying to work the knots loose. "I'm so sorry! I love you!"

"Wha—?" said Braft, suddenly awake.

"You don't have to say it back!" she rasped, having an exceedingly difficult time pulling even one knot loose. "Fuck, it," she said. "We have to go now, I'll untie you later!" And with that she grabbed his feet and began to drag him bodily up the beach, back towards his house at a surprisingly brisk pace for a small woman he clearly outweighed by at least the size of several additional small women.

"Wait, Fliz, wait," pleaded Braft, but she was driven. "Not *this* time, monster," she declared as she dragged him over the sand, pebbles, weeds, garbage and cigarette butts of the beach towards safety. Braft finally managed to free one of his hands and grabbed hold of a tree root protruding from the sand, pulling them both to a stop. "Fliz, wait..!"

"What is wrong with you!?" she cried, whirling on him. "Do you *want* to get eaten by the Edwards Lake Monster?!"

Braft considered his next words very carefully. He felt a deep shame, chiding himself for once again thinking he could use deceit as a tool to find happiness. He knew he wasn't going to be eaten by the Edwards Lake Monster because he *was* the Edwards Lake Monster. Could he tell her the truth? Would she reject him for lying? Or was love, like Fliz, truly blind?

Pangbort's Affliction

When Pangbort's date said she was hungry enough to eat a horse, the idiom went right over his head, and he ended the dinner immediately.

"I'm sorry, you have to leave," he said earnestly. "I'm vegan and I can't condone cruelty to animals."

Thinking he was joking, she laughed and replied "Oh, yes, I'm such a monster." Pangbort screamed in terror and threw himself off his own condo balcony to escape. He fell to his death, another victim of undiagnosed but very treatable metaphor-blindness.

Majesto

The assistant manager pushed the plated bagel over the counter towards her customer, a frowning older woman with grey hair. "Next in line, please," she said coldly.

"On second thought I'll take it to go," snapped the customer. "I suddenly don't feel very welcome here."

"Certainly." replied the assistant manager, curtly. She transferred the bagel to a paper bag and tossed it on the counter. "Next in line?"

"Um, excuse me," huffed the customer. "Where's my large coffee?"

"Your *majesto* will be at the counter when the barista calls your name."

"I didn't ask for a *majesto*, I asked for a *large*," said the customer, enunciating the word 'large' as two syllables. Her intent was to be an asshole, and she was nailing it.

"A *majesto* is a large," snapped the assistant manager.

"Well, that's just stupid!" eye-rolled the customer. "By that logic, this bagel is a pie and that muffin is a border collie!"

"Things can be called different things and still be the same thing!" countered the assistant manager.

"Well, if the customer is always right, why not just not call it large?!" screamed the angry woman as she dropped into a low crouch, creating a sizzling ball of crackling blue lightning between her hands. People in the queue behind her ran for cover.

"Because it's called a *majesto*!" snarled the assistant manager, tracing an arcane symbol in the air, summoning a protective shield of shimmering brimstone plasma and a whip of hissing, pulsating green energy.

"*Large!*" bellowed the woman, throwing her ball of hell at the assistant manager. It bounced off the younger woman's protective energy shield and tore a sizzling hole in the ceiling. A grown man in his thirties wearing diapers and riding a tricycle fell through the hole in the ceiling, landing in a clattering thud on the floor behind the assistant manager. "I'm alright," he said a moment later, though he did not get up.

"*Majesto!*" countered the assistant manager, snapping the old woman's glasses off her face with a crack of her sizzling whip.

"*Large!*" yelled the woman again, loading up another even larger ball of energy. The tension mounted to a feverish pitch as the two titans paused, each winded from the death energies they were conjuring, sizing each other up like cornered elemental beasts, each one willing the other to make the first mistake.

Finally, the assistant manager could take it no longer.

"Okay, fine," she hissed, her shield and whip dissipating into nothing. She pounded the counter with her fists. "Large, then!"

she hissed, scribbling furiously on a majesto cup with a marker. "Your *LARGE* coffee will be ready at the pickup counter when the barista calls your name! Are you happy now?"

"No!" shrieked the customer.

"Then what is this about?!"

"You should have married David!"

"Fuck you, mom!" hollered the assistant manager. She turned and stomped through the kitchen to the manager's office door, slamming it behind her with a gesture.

"He was a doctor!" screamed the woman at the slammed door. She began to sob inconsolably. She turned to the long line of wide-eyed customers peeking out from behind tables and chairs throughout the store. "He was a doctor," she wailed miserably, looking for a kind look, a nod of understanding, for someone, anything to console her.

"*Large Bitch*?" called the barista from the pick-up counter, reading the name scrawled in Sharpie on the cup of coffee he'd just made. "*Majesto* for *Large Bitch*?"

Butterfly Knife

oazie Knalch rolled her SUV to a stop half a block up the street from *Yes You CanVenience*. She'd never been in the store before, but she'd driven by many times and had admired the colourful fruit and beautiful flower arrangements on display outside.

She looked at the time on the dashboard display; she was a bit early before meeting her clients at the open house just around the corner. She paid for parking on her phone, straightened her suit jacket, took a deep breath, and walked with purpose towards the store. She was distracted momentarily by the beautiful wildflowers on someone's front lawn. No one else was on the street; she knew she could probably grab them without getting caught, but she thought better of it and kept walking.

At the storefront she eyed the fragrant bouquets for sale in the plastic buckets, but when she noticed the watchful young clerk with multicoloured hair inside the shop keeping an eye on her through the window, she grew self-conscious and hesitant. A little boy raced up on a bike, skidded to a stop in front of her, threw his bike to the ground and ran inside ahead of her. She realized she shouldn't just steal these flowers after all, but she didn't really want any other customers in the store when she paid for them, so she waited, pretending to text and scroll until the kid came wheezing back out with a bag of junk food as big as his torso. As he pedalled wobblingly away, she walked in.

She smiled at the clerk as she walked past the counter; they nodded back to her glumly as she disappeared down the aisle, then looked up to watch her on the surveillance monitors. Moazie meandered up and down every aisle, picking up random items as though she had a list, when really she just making sure nobody else was in the store. A minute later she casually placed a roll of packing tape, a tub of Haagen-Dazs, a bag of cheezies, a can of creamed corn and a box of condoms on the counter.

"Oh, yeah, these, too," said Moazie, handing the clerk a handful of gum packs from the counter display. She also grabbed two fidget spinners and three copies of the same Archie Comics Digest issue. "These too, and, yeah, I'll grab some smokes, too. As well, I mean. Also. I'll grab two smokes, also."

The clerk nodded towards the cigarette display. "What kind?"

"Surprise me," said Moazie.

"Okay," replied the clerk, grabbing a random pack and scanning them.

"Got any papers?" asked Moazie.

"Like newspapers? For reading?"

"Rolling paper. For smoking. You know. For weed?" she smirked. "I'm old but I still like to party."

"Okay. Plain or flavour?"

"What kind do you like?" she asked.

The cashier shrugged. "I don't smoke."

"Gimme one of each flavour, then, and actually, you know what? Take back the smokes and just make it a whole can of tobacco. Who needs filters, amiright? I'm gonna die someday so I might as well live a little. Oh, and one of those Bic lighters."

"Kay."

"Four, actually. I'm always losing them."

"Kay."

"You got any of those glass-blown bowls? The crack pipe-looking ones?" The clerk pointed at the display of glass pipes in plain sight right next to her on the counter.

"Pfft. Geez, right here in front of me," said Moazie, rolling her eyes. "Ha. Lucky it wasn't a wasps' nest, right?"

"I guess."

"Ooh, pretty," she said, spying one of the pipes that had an attractive bit of a white, yellow and orange swirl to it. "Really catches the eye." She grabbed that one and put it in her mouth. She did a few practice pulls on it, looking the opposite of what she hoped was not awkward. For some reason one of the pipes with a bit more purple spoke to her, so she handed the clerk that one and put the orange one back.

"Uh. You just put your mouth on the other one and put it back," said the clerk.

"Oh. Is that a health code thing?"

"Well."

"Fine, I'll take them both."

As the clerk scanned the two glass pipes, Moazie's heart jumped as her eye fell across the knife display case. There were some standard pocket knives and switchblades, a few clichéd Rambo-style hunting knives, along with some very dangerous looking serrated street knives. She waited till she knew she had her breath under control, then she winked at the clerk.

"Those legal?" she asked with a knowing smile.

"I don't know."

"Lemme see that one," said Moazie, pointing at a matte black butterfly knife. The clerk found the key to the display, opened it, and handed it over to Moazie. "D'you like this one?" she asked, testing the weight in her hand.

"Sure," mumbled the clerk.

"Did you know they originated in the Philippines?"

"No."

"Quick. Discrete. Lethal." she said, tossing the knife high up into the air behind her back. She then did a standing back-flip, expertly catching the knife again as it dropped. Flicking the blade open in one deft move, she then launched into an impressive kata, expertly swooshing the knife around in the air, back and forth, darting in and out as she showcased various killing strokes. "Y'ever wonder why they call them butterfly knives?"

"No."

"No, of course not, why would you ever?" said Moazie, her voice now a dark whisper as her eyes narrowed and locked with the clerk's. Their eyes dilated slightly, as though they were sharing a sudden intoxication. "They're coming," said Moazie, and the air between them attained an almost sexual weight. Dazed, the clerk leaned in closer to her, and closer still. They were interrupted when a pair of kids burst into the store, a flurry of stomping feet and outdoor voices that giggled and huffed their way to the candy aisle.

"What?" said the clerk, shaking their head slightly.

"Nothing, nothing," said Moazie hurriedly. "Those kids, I meant. They're coming, I saw them coming. They're here, I mean, that's what I meant." She flicked the blade shut and brought her hands together in a deep bow to the clerk. "Konichiwa," she said, solemnly placing it on her now immense pile of purchases.

"Racist," muttered the clerk in that morally indignant way young adults have when they sense a social wrong. "Culturally appropriative, at best," muttered Moazie, in that defensive tone older people have when they are technically correct but still kind of being shitty. The clerk indicated the total on the register. "How do you wanna pay?"

"Visa. Oh, pfft, almost forgot," she lied, acting (badly) like it was an afterthought and not the original reason she was in here. "Charge me for one of those wildflower arrangements outside, oh, I don't know, oh, pfft, one of the large purplish ones, the big one, third from the left? Is that lavender?"

"I don't know," shrugged the clerk, adding the flowers to the total. After getting her pin number wrong twice, Moazie paid and carried her bags to the door, which she nonchalantly opened with her butt. Once outside she grabbed the bouquet as casually as possible in case the clerk was still watching (which they were not) and walked up the street.

Once she knew she was out of sight of the storefront, a clammy sweat broke out on her brow, and she picked up the pace, thinking only about the knife she'd just bought. Arriving at her parking spot, she hesitated, lost in conflict and indecision. She shook her head and tried to focus.

A few seconds later, she threw both bags of purchases into a municipal garbage can and climbed behind the wheel and privacy of her tinted windows with only the bouquet of flowers still clutched in her hand. Her whole body began to tremble as she held the bouquet up to her face

She gagged once, twice, and then her eyes went blank. Her

mouth stretched open as far as it could go, till her jaw itself unhinged and the top of her head dropped back like a broken Pez dispenser. From deep inside her throat, a mutated monarch butterfly with a body as big as a human fist clambered up onto her tongue, flicking and airing out its wet wings. Several small larvae skittered around her, joining in the feast as her proboscis darted ravenously over the sweet nectar of the milkwood and lavender feast Moazie held before them in her motionless hands.

Once fed, the mother and her spawn retreated back to the warm folds of her throat, and Moazie's head returned to its normal position. She rubbed her jaw as her eyes cleared and conscious thought slowly returned. *"Thank you,"* she heard a voice say in her mind. *"Fed am We. You serve We well."*

"I hear. I obey. I tend to the needs of the swarm," she thought.

"So say you," came the reply, in a tone as stifling as a weighted blanket. *"But Moazie?"*

"Yes?"

"You seek to end We with butterfly knife? You try to send warning to young human drone inside the convenience store?"

"Forgive me," replied Moazie, a knot forming in her stomach.

"Forgive, yes," replied her parasitic occupant. *"Forget? No. The Great Swarm approaches. You try such again? We find new host so fast your head explode."*

"I understand, Blessed Hovering Harbinger," gulped Moazie.

"That not euphemism. Kaboom. No test We."

"Yes, your orange-winged greatness."

"This good chat," said the butterfly-thing, satisfied in her host's obeisance for the moment. *"Time is two of your clocks, yes? Appointment you have with the Andersons. Let us go. My hatchlings must needs find new nesting."*

Moazie got out of the car in a daze and began to trudge towards the house around the corner. Maybe it wouldn't be so horrific this time. She'd soon have to actually sell this house before it really got suspicious at the office, but for now, maybe if she could warn the Andersons somehow? Or maybe if she could keep them near an open window where there could be witnesses...

"Pick up feet. This time, you no scream when my larvae take them, yes? Smile, Moazie, smile! Remember: evolve or die. And also location, location, location!"

Jorsch

When Grace asked Jorsch why he appeared to be a sentient pineapple (and not an attractive human male as she'd been led to believe by the photo on his online profile) Jorsch hesitated.

Did she care that he had been human, once?

Would she be intrigued by the story of how, as a child, he had always wondered why the instructions on the package of jello always explicitly mentioned you should never add pineapples, but never explained why?

Would she understand how his insatiable desire led to his conducting highly unethical experiments that bridged the boundaries between man and fruit?

Would she agree that he had paid the price for his hubris in the lab accident, or should he indulge himself with the long-winded, academic explanation that he craved to launch into, but which had ended so many previous dates?

"I'm rich," he said, instead.

"I'm listening," she said.

Father's Day

Father's Day at my house was always the same.

We'd give Dad his cards and make him breakfast, then he'd ask us if we wanted to learn another one of our "family secrets."

Over the years, we had learned our family secrets had a common theme: that when you pulled Dad's finger, a magical noise happened. (Sometimes that noise had a bad smell.) We had discovered that when you squeezed Dad's nose, a magical noise happened. (Sometimes that noise had a bad smell.) We had discovered that when you pulled Dad's ear, a magical noise happened. (Sometimes that noise had a bad smell.)

Last Father's Day, my younger brother, who has kids of his own now and was tired of learning secrets, said "Dad...? Got any secrets that aren't just farts?"

At that point, my dad looked at us and smiled wistfully. "You have learned all I have taught you. I have no secrets left to keep," he said, and turned into a pillar of sand.

My niece and nephew screamed for hours, but that pillar of sand gag is still my dad's best work.

Gettin' Spaghetti

From their perch atop a wooden beam twelve feet above the floor of Mamma Linguini's Ristorante, Repp and Julp watched as Don Vito Genovese was served the biggest plate of fresh spaghetti and meatballs they had ever seen.

"You sure no one can see us, Repp?" whispered Julp, his voice just a whisper below the din of Sinatra blasting from the transistor radio.

"Sure, I'm sure," replied Repp. "Now here's the plan. I got this fork tied around this beam with this rope. You gotta run to the end of the beam, and you jump off and hold on. This'll create the perfect parabola and you'll swing down there, nab all that spaghetti with this fork, then you'll swing back up here and we'll eat like kings!"

Julp was skeptical. "You sure it can hold me?"

"Sure, I'm sure." replied Repp.

"Why am I the one jumping?"

"Because I'm the ideas guy and I already did the math for the parabola using your weight and the length of the rope I tied the fork to," said Repp.

"You sure *parabola* means what you think it means?" asked Julp.

And so it went. They'd been hoarsely debating the finer points of compass geometry and tensile strengths for nearly five minutes when Don Vito looked up and cleared his throat.

Everybody in the restaurant froze. Repp and Julp pinched each other's lips shut and looked down, wide-eyed. Mama Linguini apprehensively scurried over to attend to him. "Yes, Don Vito?" she asked reverently.

"I think I would like a little change in ambience," was all he said.

"Si, Don Vito, si!" said Mama Linguini. She turned towards the staff, clapped her hands and made a cutting motion across her throat with her thumb. "Pssst! Ambiance!"

One of Mama Linguini's nephews rushed to dim the lights as a half-dozen orphans emerged from multiple hiding places and hurriedly lit candles on all the other tables throughout the restaurant. Her other nephew with the overbite turned off the radio while her second cousin from Sicily (not the one you're thinking of but the musician) emerged from the broom closet with an elegant, mahogany violin. He stepped briskly to Don Vito's side and began to play.

"There you are, Don Vito," smiled Mama Linguini, kissing his ring. "A change of ambiance. Special for you." A mollified Don Vito smiled and nodded his approval as he resumed his meal. But Julp and Repp had now hit a snag.

"C-C-Candles," whispered Julp, his eyes aglow.

"Cheese it," said Repp. "I hadn't counted on c-c-candles…"

Mesmerized, all thoughts of pasta behind them, Repp and Julp threw themselves off the beam and fluttered towards Don Vito's table. Upon touching the bewitching flames of the candle, they were both burnt to ash. And so ended the adventures of Julp and Repp, the two smartest moths on the Lower East Side.

Le Coureur Des Bois

The doorbell rang and Clinch Wasp assumed it was the Mormons again, but when he opened the door to shoo them away, he found himself looking at a short, glowering and unkempt seventeenth century *coureur des bois*.

"*Hé*, remember me, *tête carré*?!" growled the wild-eyed French-Canadian woodsman. Before Clinch could respond, the pungent little man had blown into a small tube, shooting a poison dart that embedded itself into Clinch's neck with a sharp airy *whoosh*.

Clinch's eyes bulged, and his entire body froze, ramrod straight. Gravity pulled him forward slowly, and he timbered off the porch with a single, rigored grunt. His body rolled over several times before coming to an uncomfortable stop on his face.

"At last I find you, *maudit anglais*!" cried the *coureur des bois*, pushing Clinch onto his back with his foot. The hirsute little anachronism clapped his hands and stamped his feet in a little jig as he pulled a fiddle and bow out of his long, shaggy beard. "Hee, hee, hee, *tiguidou*!" he laughed, launching into a lively reel as he sang along triumphantly. "A-deedly, deedly, deedly-doo, a-deedly, deedly --"

Inside his immobile skull, Clinch's mind raced. Had he fallen asleep in history class, or was he correct that poison blow darts were somewhat atypical of *coureur de bois* paraphernalia? He tried to speak, but could only manage a schlupping, inquisitive groan.

Still, it was enough to get the man-badger's attention. The *coureur des bois* stopped fiddling and leaned over Clinch's face.

"*Hein, quoi, mon ostie?*" he growled.

"Mwahaugh," said Clinch.

"You never see me before, you say? Me neither, I never see you before, but I know 'ou you har!"

"Bllwuaaaugh?"

"Good question!" he laughed, lifting his arms to the sky, fiddle in one hand, bow in the other. A flock of chattering, blue-black ravens swirled around him, and the ground began to shake. "I am Saint Jean-Guy Charlesvoix D'Ayoille Déguelasse," he bellowed as a bolt of lightning struck his bow and he glowed and crackled with power. "*Coureur des bois!*" An owl hooted, a wolf howled, and then… silence. Then, he resumed his fiddling taunt-dance. "A deedly deedly deedly dee--"

Although thoroughly impressed with the supernatural vignette he'd just witnessed, Clinch still had questions, and he struggled to make them fall out of his frozen face. Again, the *coureur des bois* stopped fiddling and leaned in. "*Hein, quoi, mon câlis?*"

"Buhmah cungnghfews…"

"Oh, you are *confusé?*"

Clinch mouth-gurgled in agreement.

"*Ouais, bien*, I will *deconfusé* you!" continued Jean-Guy. With a finger-snap, he transformed the fiddle into a wooden stump on which he sat down. "Okay, *mon calvaire*," he said, pulling out a tobacco pouch and rolling himself a smoke. "*Bien*, once upon a time, *la*, I was a trapper in Nouvelle France. It was the year of our Lord 1670 and I work very 'ard to trap beaver fur and pelt so I can trade for my living."

He paused to strike a match off of Clinch's forehead, lit his cigarette and continued. "I have big dreams of saving enough to buy land one day, have a small farm and make many French-Canadian *habitants* children with a lusty or available French-Canadian lover-woman or womens.

"So me, I catch a lot of fur and pelt, but one night I go to sleep, and I wake up and there is all my fur! Gone! Some *enfant de chienne* stole my fur and pelt in the night! So I go paddle fast like the wind to the trade outpost, but I am too late. The man there tell me, someone comes just before and sell so many beaver pelt and fur. He say they never see him before, and they don't see where he go. But they say, he was some big *maudit anglais*."

Jean-Guy blew a huge cloud of smoke through his nostrils, looking demonic as his glaring eyes narrowed and fixed on Clinch. "That big *maudit anglais* was your *grand grand grand grand grand grand grand grand grand grand grand grandpére*....you understand me? *Tu comprends?*"

Clinch was silent. Jean-Guy translated. "I mean, that big damn

English was your great great great great great great great great great great great great grandfa --"

Clinch interrupted with a series of jabbered protestations, but Jean-Guy was having none of it. "*Ta guelle, ostie,*" he tsked. "You will hear my exposition! Where was I? Euh… *simonac*, you make me lose my place!"

Jean-Guy went through his mental setlist. "Okay, 1670, stolen fur, lusty womens, blah blah blah… ah, yes! *Oauis*, okay, so, my furs are all stole by the *maudit anglais*, your ancestor, and me, I don't know why this *enfant d'ostie* steal from me! I don't do nothing to him! So, me, I'm very 'urt by this.

"But also I'm so angry! I work so hard and now I have nothing! And I think to myself, I say, why me, God? So I fall to my knees and I look up and I blame God. I shake my fist and I cry so hard and I scream and I blame him for all my suffering. But God? He hear me, and he is *très fâché, hein*? He is very pissed off after me, *blasphème*!

"And den a big piece of lightning shoot me where I stand. Kapow, *ostie*! I explode fast away from my shoes and I land hupstairs in a tree and I go to sleep a long time. When I wake up, I hear His voice and he tell me 'Allo, bonjour. Wake up. You sleep okay? This is God. I make you sleep in a tree to teach you a lesson. I work in a mysterious ways so now I gonna make you a saint. *Boum*! Like that!

"Now you are gonna be called Saint Jean-Guy Charlevoix D'Ayoille Déguelasse, patron saint of lost fur hats! Anywhere someone lose a fur hat, he tells me, the believers gonna pray to you for help to find it, and you will tell them where. This is a big gift I give you to serve me, but also still I gonna put on you a big penance. You gonna never die, *hein*? *Immortel.*

"Now you go wander the earth. And you help everyone find their hats. But every *anniversaire* of this day, you must tell your story to a descendant of the *maudit anglais* who stole your beaver furs…" And here, Jean-Guy paused, for dramatic effect. He pointed a finger at Clinch. "This year, *c'est toi*. It's you."

"Whaaught?" gurgled Clinch, skeptically.

"*C'est vrai*, it's true!" snapped Jean-Guy. "For over 300 years, once a year, I find someone like you, a descendant of the *maudit anglais* who stole my -- !" Clinch throat-grunted an inquisitive interruption.

"What you asking me, *gros colon*?" Jean-Guy listened carefully as Clinch repeated himself, then huffed with irritation. "I learn about shooting poison blow dart on Discovery channel, like everyone else, *ostie*. So many questions! All about you!" Jean-Guy sat back down on his stump and rolled himself a new smoke.

Clinch gurgled indignantly; he was the one lying on the ground under the influence of who knows what kind of toxin, why shouldn't it be about him?

"Oh, yeah, tough guy?" said Jean-Guy as he poked Clinch in the forehead with an accusatory finger. "*Monsieur* big shot? You have somewhere to go, *hein*? Well, too bad for you, den, I don't gonna tell you how I discover gold, how I create *poutine*, which place you lost your fur hat, or about the weekend Jerry Garcia teach me how to play punch-buggy. Many good stories, but you don't get to hear them. *Eh, bien. C'est la vie.*"

With the new smoke lit and hanging off his lower lip, Jean-Guy then produced a large crucifix from his rucksack. Tied to the crucifix, in place of Jesus, was a racoon tail. "And now, by the power of this cross from the parish of the *cul de sac* D'Ayoille Déguelasse, I gonna pray your immortal soul into this racoon tail, and I gonna keep it with me forever!"

Clinch protested, but Jean-Guy was determined. He stuck the cross into the ground. He took off his shoes to reveal rosary beads tied around each ankle. Then he stood, and the stump immediately leapt into his hands and transformed back into a fiddle. Jean-Guy's eyes rolled back into his head and he began to play a feverishly fast-paced and demonic-sounding reel, all the while muttering a litany of Lord's Prayers and Hail Mary's while counting out the rosary beads with his toes.

Sparks flew off the raccoon tail, every hair of it standing on end, till it jumped to life, racing to the end of its string like a chained dog, hissing and screeching an inch from Clinch's face. Clinch began to gibber in fear as he felt something… a weight, a presence, a sensation of something being pulled out of himself and into the raccoon tail.

Clinch began screaming in earnest, hitting notes he'd never reached before, even when he was in the boys choir. His piercing wail broke through Jean-Guy's concentrated praying. "*Mange de la merde, mon crisse,*" he yelled. "You make me lose my place!"

The racoon tail, annoyed at the interruption of its soul meal, began yowling in protest. Jean-Guy hissed and stamped his feet at it. "Psst! *Hé! Tais-toi.* Go lay down! *Va te coucher!*" The racoon tail whimpered and scampered to perch on its cross where, though it didn't have eyes, it glared at Clinch as scornfully as an undead racoon tail could.

Clinch began babbling again, looking at Jean-Guy with pleading eyes. "*C'est quoi encore?*" said Jean-Guy, leaning closer to Clinch's face. "It hurt more when you interrupt me. What you want?"

"Aughew thoor thith ithin amythtake?"

"A mistake?" Jean-Guy paused, almost empathetically. "Fate makes no mistakes, *mon pauvre p'tit bonhomme.* It's not my fault, *hein*? Its destiny, *câlis.* Hits an eye for an eye, toot for a toot, it's in the *sainte bible, ostie.*"

"Augh ewe thoor thoor?"

"Am I sure sure? Ouais, I'm sure, sure, *tête de pioche,*" replied Jean-Guy. "You need more proof? Okay, I gonna prove you, *ostie.*" He snapped his fingers, and his fiddle turned into an iPhone. Tapping a few buttons, he stared at the screen myopically. "Tsk, too small, *tabarnac,*" he muttered, turning his back to self-consciously pull out a pair of reading glasses. He peered down his nose at the screen. "Okay, *mon niaseux,*" said Jean-Guy, scrolling through his contacts list. "This is 145 Tweedsmuir Court, *non?*"

"*Non!*" rasped Clinch, glad at this moment he'd been forced to take grade nine French.

"What you mean, *non*?" said Jean-Guy. "You mean *non*, this is <u>not</u> 145 Tweedsmuir Court?"

"*Oui!*" rasped Clinch emphatically.

"*Oui*, it is <u>not</u> 145 Tweedsmuir Court?"

"Oui!"

Jean-Guy looked over at the porch and could clearly see the address above the door: 147 Tweedsmuir Court. He looked back at Clinch, puzzled.

"*Mais quand même*, your name is Harsh Malmgord, non?"

"Non!"

"You mean, *non*, your name is not Harsh Malmgord?"

"Oui!"

Jean-Guy's shoulders slumped as he sighed. "Ah, *bien, vierge de crisse*," he said, every line in his face showing the exhaustion of all three hundred and more years of his unending curse. He cleared his throat and put away his glasses and for a long moment, said nothing. Then he clapped his hands and smiled cordially. "*Ah, bien. J'm'excuse.* Wrong *adresse,* wrong *tête carré.* You can't get it right every year, *hein? Eh, bien,* I go now."

The *coureur des bois* tapped on his phone, and at the end of the walk in front of Clinch's house, a canoe appeared in a puff of campfire-smelling smoke. He untied the racoon tail from the crucifix, and it immediately scurried up to Clinch and began nuzzling his nose affectionately. "The raccoon tail now contains most of your soul. I release it to you. Take good care of it, *hein?* If you feel cold, she feels cold, so she sleeps inside at night, okay, *mon crisse?*"

Jean-Guy then knelt down in front of Clinch and did the sign of the cross. "I absolve you of your sins of being *une crisse de tête carré.* You will regain full use of your body in a few hours." Then he took a huge backwards leap in the air and landed in the canoe. "*Au revoir, mon ostie!*" he cried, as he paddled away into the twilight sky, shrinking till he was nothing but a small dot, and then into nothing at all.

In a few hours, just as the mystical *coureur des bois* had promised, Clinch did regain control of his body. He brought the raccoon tail into his home, and over the years, it gave Clinch some very solid investment advice, and the two of them lived comfortably to a very old age.

Country Road

I could hear the mournful a cappella voice well before I even turned the corner. "Country rooooad... take me hooome..."

Half a block down I spied the singer, a scruffy, disheveled man about sixty years old. He was really leaning into his performance, as if the stoop where he stood was the grandest amphitheatre, his voice booming out over the traffic and bustle of Queen Street, a man of longing and heartache, alone against the urban wilderness. "To the plaaace... I belooong..."

He didn't look like he'd had a meal or a bath in a while, and I meant to walk right past him, but something in the raw emotion of his voice made me stop and listen. "West Virginiaaa..."

I found myself hard-pressed to imagine this probably homeless guy had ever been to either of the Virginias, then I shamefully checked myself. I didn't know his life story. I didn't know why he'd fallen on hard times, or if he'd always lived like this. Maybe he chose this life, and even if he hadn't, I was no better than him, maybe just luckier. Who was I to judge him, just another human being, trying to get by in Toronto, same as me?

I felt a quiet empathy for him. Who knows how many places he'd been, or the things he'd seen, the chances he'd had and the hard knocks he'd endured?

"Mountain mommaaaa..." he wailed, and I, too, ached for a simpler, quieter place and time.

"Take me home…" Yeah. Home would be nice, I thought, as I dropped a couple bucks in his hat and pictured the rolling hills of my home, the northwestern stretch of the Saint John River valley in rural New Brunswick, the place where I belonged…

"Country rooooad…"

He closed his eyes as he held the last, long, plaintive note, then bowed his head for a moment. Then he looked at me and nodded. "Thanks, brother," he said. "Everything helps."

"Big John Denver fan?" I asked.

He shook his head. "Nope." In the blink of an eye, a burst of smoke rose from a crack in the sidewalk, materializing into the ghost of American singer-songwriter, activist and humanitarian John Denver.

The bespectacled apparition kicked the busker in the nuts, grabbing all the money in the hat as the man grunted and hit the ground at the same time as my mouth fell open. "Yoink!" jeered the spectre, giving us both the finger as it turned back into an ethereal fume that siphoned back into the sidewalk from where it had come.

"Aw, don't worry about me. He ain't so bad, I guess," muttered the busker, sitting up to catch his breath. "Plus, another forty bucks, and he says he'll give my guitar back."

Aisle Four

L arynx was pricing cans of stewed tomatoes in aisle four when he heard the noise.

Although he had very limited short term memory, even compared to his parents, he dimly remembered having heard it before, and it made him frown. He didn't like how it was making him feel, so he took a deep breath and tried to ignore it by just focusing on his work.

He loved his work.

He loved losing himself in the steady, lulling click-schlupp sound of the price gun. Other employees might feel this sort of menial task beneath them, but not Larynx. The noise of the gun helped him ignore all the other background noises, pressures and anxieties that made up the mind-numbing banality of his adolescence. It helped him cope with all the other things he didn't know how to deal with, like the disappointment of his parents, alienation from his peers, and the crush he was developing on that cute new cashier.

He became so engaged in his work that when he heard the noise again, it caught him fully by surprise. He stood up straight, the pricing gun paused in mid-schlupp. "What was that?" he wondered dimly, having forgotten that he'd heard it a moment earlier, and several times before that, for the last twenty minutes.

He listened intently. And there it was again. Now where was it coming from?

He turned to his left. Nothing. He cocked his head and turned to the right. Nothing.

And there it was again.

Was it coming from the front of the store? Forgetting that the noise had made him frown earlier, he trudged up to the end of aisle four to investigate.

From there, he could see all ten register lanes. As usual, only three cashiers were scheduled, with a growing line of impatient customers waiting to be served. It was a terrible way to treat patrons, he thought, not to speak of the staff. If he were the manager, there would be changes… but then why would he ever become a manager when it would take him away from his sticker gun duties? He supposed if he were manager he could keep the sticker gun duties for himself, but the thought of extra duties and responsibility began to make him anxious, till he was distracted from his malaise by the noise he'd once again forgotten about.

This time, however, Layrnx realized that he was the one making the noise. It was coming from his abdomen, to be exact, and it was growing louder.

Was he… hungry?

He didn't think so, and yet, he couldn't remember the last time he'd eaten… and that was his last conscious thought. By now the customers themselves could hear him and they turned, wide-eyed, to where Larynx stood at the top of aisle four.

His six eyes glowed hot white, and he trembled and shook as his mouth fell open and he took a shambling, almost drunken step forward as the Hunt Sleep (that he would promptly forget) once again took hold of him.

The cashiers dropped for cover and the building shook as multiple psychic tendrils shot out from his abdomen. They turned the interior organic matter of every customer they touched into multicoloured bands of pure cellular energy that blasted out from their every orifice. This maelstrom of essential nutrients snaked through the air and gathered in a thunderous storm cloud of light ribbons above him, and then, one by one, each strand funnelled into his slurping mouth like photonic spaghetti. He feasted ravenously till his hunger was appeased.

When it was over, consciousness returned to him, and he stood there, sweating and blinking dumbly as the lifeless and empty non-ingestible skin bag remains of his victims slowly burned out like paper lanterns, wafting to the ground into tiny piles, each weighing twenty-one grams.

Feeling satiated and newly confident, Larynx saw the pretty cashier he liked as she stood up from her hiding place.

"Hey," he said.

"Hey," she replied.

"You wanna hang out Saturday night?" he said.

"Uh, no, I have a thing..?" she said.

"Okay," he said, and trudged back to finish his can-pricing down aisle four, where he forgot everything that had just happened.

From his second floor loft office overlooking the store, branch manager Dubious Runtzle frowned and flipped the blinds shut. Great, he thought, another whole day of responding to a social media shitstorm, but there was no way he was going to fire Larynx. Nobody worked harder than a Gambalorian Energy Feeder, and for less than minimum wage at that. Sure, you'd lose a few customers a few times a month, but at these prices? They'd be back.

Red Buttons

Marfinsh stared at the red button on the inside of his front door.

It hadn't been there when he'd left for work this morning, but now, as he arrived home, punctual as a bean at 5:36 pm, there it was. This was the first time he'd seen a red button inside his own home. He wished he were surprised, but he wasn't.

He'd been noticing similar buttons for a few years.

At first it was just one or two a week. He might notice one attached to a transit shelter and give it no thought. Then a few days later he might see one on a city trash can. He thought maybe it was some sort of ad campaign for… well, red buttons, he assumed, or some other marketing gimmick aimed so far above his head and outside of his demographic that he didn't expect to understand it.

Within a matter of months he was seeing them daily on trees, hydrants, cars, convenience store sandwiches; everywhere. Still, he'd taken it all in stride, until he realized nobody else could see them.

He tried several times to point out red buttons to passersby, but they would look at him sideways or, more often, simply ignore him. Coworkers humoured him at first when he pointed out the red button on the coffee maker. "Red button? You're a red button," they'd joked. "Red button, right," they'd said. "Must be

Monday." Soon, they would change the subject or start avoiding or ignoring him, too, so he just stopped pointing them out.

"Babe?" he asked his wife one evening. "Have you noticed any red buttons lately?" Without looking away from Jeff Probst she replied, "No, but he was very good in *Poseidon Adventure*."

And as he stood here now, staring at the red button on the inside of his front door, a thought struck him that drained the colour from his face. He wondered what would happen if he pushed it? If he *was* the only person who could see them, he reasoned, wasn't it his responsibility… to *push* one?

His heart began to beat faster and his chest tightened. He could feel his arm rising, his hand turning into a fist, his index finger extending to a fine button-pushing point. His breath came in ragged gasps. Sweat trickled down his brow.

He pushed the red button. It clicked. It turned yellow. Marfinsh held his breath. And then nothing else happened.

He wasn't sure what he'd been expecting but surely something more than this? He waited by the door another twenty minutes till his wife called him in for dinner. He tried to make conversation, he tried to stay positive, he tried to enjoy *Show Me Your Voice*, but he went to bed grumpy, turning the day's events over and over in his mind until he fell asleep fitfully.

As he prepared to leave for work at exactly 8:35 the next morning, the yellow button was still there on the back of the door. What did it want? Was it mocking him? His cheeks flushed as an irrational anger grew within him. He snarled, and in a two-minute long temper tantrum, he pressed the button again and again until the tempest had passed.

He sighed with relief and checked his watch. It was now 8:37 and he had to be on his way, but his breath hitched and his heart leapt into his throat. The button had turned green.

He waited. He would be late, but he was rooted to the spot in fear. But nothing else happened. Finally, after seven minutes, he shrugged. "Green means go," he supposed, so off he went.

He saw many red buttons on his swifter-than-usual walk to work that morning. Some had of course been there for months, but there were also many new ones in new locations. They were all still red, not yellow or green, and just like before, nobody else seemed to notice them. He'd always been fine with the buttons before, but today, he began to feel a sense of unease. "What to do," he began to fret, till he very literally began to panic about what to do.

He felt like the brunt of some cruel long-game joke, very small and alone. He reasoned, reasonably enough, that there was a wide spectrum of sane, acceptable human behaviour. Some people were afraid of snakes, some people were liars, some people hated vegetables, some people were exhibitionists; maybe he was just some guy who saw red buttons? Sweat broke out on his brow and he forced himself to just… keep… walking… but every red button on his trip brought up more questions that he struggled to answer.

Was he a danger to other people? No, not that he could tell.

Was this phenomenon of red buttons life-altering? Not really. Was there anything he could do about it? He didn't think so.

He remembered a quote misattributed many times to Einstein: "Insanity is doing the same thing over and over again and expecting a different result." He wasn't about to spend the rest of his life pushing every red button he saw if all it did was turn them yellow and sometimes green. That truly would be insanity. And somehow knowing that he was in control of whether he pushed buttons or not calmed him down a little.

Nobody noticed when he slipped quietly behind his desk at the office a few minutes late and very sweaty; both attributes that were very unlike him. Instead, everyone was talking about the breaking news from Topeka, Kansas. It seemed that the Westboro Baptist Church had been swallowed by a sinkhole the night before, around 5:36 pm. His stomach sank. That was when the red button on his door had turned yellow. And then this morning, between 8:35 and 8:37 am, as he'd been punching the yellow button, every single member of the church had turned into a pillar of salt. And then the button had turned green. Coincidence?

Marfinsh knew it wasn't.

That night, he lay wide awake, feeling alone and very small, his wife snoring softly beside him, blissfully unaware of the hesitant hero her husband had become.

Nesmith & the Sheriff

Nesmith had a very specific phobia. It was ridiculous, really, but none of his very expensive therapists had heard of anything like it.

Nesmith was afraid his bed would become a time-portal from which an old western sheriff would appear on a white stallion. The sheriff would resemble Sam Elliot, only with the body of an ostrich. In addition to its vest, badge and six-gun holsters, it would be wearing platform shoes; the kind with tiny goldfish bowls in the heels. The ostrich would ask him for directions, whereupon Nesmith would panic.

He would grab the sheriff by the neck and pull it bodily down from the saddle. Startled, the horse would neigh in fear and retreat back from where it had come through the portal. Nesmith would then bludgeon the hapless law-bird to death.

Overcome by guilt, Nesmith would cover the body with a quilt before summoning the police to his home to turn himself in. However, upon investigation they would not find a body. Given the evidence present, they would conclude that Nesmith had simply shat the bed while having a bad dream. The story would go viral and to escape the onslaught of public ridicule he'd have to get a new identity in a new town.

His fear stemmed from an overactive imagination, he knew. Still, it had happened once before, and once shitten, twice shy.

The Shadow People

Hoof Torps had first become aware of them when he was only a baby; those furtive little shadows flitting about inside the walls, floors and ceilings of his house, always just outside his peripheral vision. They were the Shadow People, and they were a near constant presence for the first years of his life.

He'd tried many times to attract their attention and interact with them, but they seemed unaware or ambivalent about his existence. But he could always seem them, whether playing in the living room with his toys, or taking a bath, or eating in the kitchen. They'd flutter in and out from under picture frames or light switches and plugs, but if he tried to look directly at them, they'd scoot just outside of his field of vision.

He used to play a little game, first in his crib and years later in his racecar bed. He pretended to be asleep, but would keep one eye slightly open. He hoped if they thought he was unconscious, they'd drop their guard and he could get a good look at them, but he always fell asleep well before that ever happened.

He mentioned them once to his parents. They smiled and told him about 'guardian angels' but this didn't feel like what they described at all. No, these things didn't really seem to care about him at all. When he asked a few close friends in elementary school if they'd ever seen anything like them, their dubious looks and snickering comments about imaginary friends made him feel awkward. To save face, he joined them in having a laugh at himself, and he never shared the experience with anyone again.

Like any secret you have to hide from others, he grew resentful of the Shadow People, and little by little he began to block them out. He ignored their gossamer comings and goings, willing them to go away and leave him alone. He simply refused to acknowledge them any longer, and he saw and heard them less and less, till eventually he neither saw nor thought of them at all.

Twenty years went by.

Then, in March of 2021, on the first anniversary of the coronavirus pandemic quarantine in Toronto, Hoof stepped off the treadmill in the small but cozy gym of his condo building. He took slow deep breaths as he adjusted his N95 and sat down on the bench press.

A neighbour who'd noticed him around the building was stretching on a mat about six feet away. She thought he was cute, at least the top part of his face was, and she'd tried for weeks to get him to notice her by doing stretches and kegels next to him whenever she could. They'd never so much as spoken but she'd always pursued emotionally unavailable guys, so she didn't think for a minute that he was just too depressed to notice her. She just thought he was playing hard to get.

His eyes glazed over, and in that two foot dead stare of mental exhaustion, something fluttered across his peripheral vision… and in that moment Hoof's memories of the Shadow People came flooding back. His heart began to pound, but he kept his eyes unfocused and steadied his breathing.

Was he dreaming? Hallucinating? Maybe all this cardio with a mask on wasn't good for him after all? But no, there it was again, definitely a shadow inside the wall, directly in front of him. And to his growing wonder, he could see the walls of the room were crawling with them, fluttering like moths. But unlike the shadows of his childhood, these shapes and shades did not retreat when he looked directly at them; instead they seemed to gather in clumps wherever his gaze landed. As though they were the ones now looking to get his attention? Were they looking for him? Were they trying to communicate? Why now, he thought, and the resentment rose in him again.

"I can see you!" he said aloud. Quite loudly. He'd hollered it, in fact, and the sudden verbalization startled a fart out of the cute neighbour who was still trying to make eye contact with him. She left the gym immediately, embarrassed beyond words. She would put her condo up for sale the next day, but that's another story.

Hoof was now surrounded on all sides by Shadow People. As though some psychic levee had broken, he now heard their voices, washing over him in waves, their thoughts rushing into his head as each one speaking pulsed and glowed in a primary colour.

"Hey. That guy said he could see us."

"Who?"

"That guy outside the wall."

"Oh!"

"Yes, that's him!"

"He's all grown!"

"Well it's about time!"

"They do take so long to mature."

"You sure he's the one we speak of in prophecy?"

"Yes, I'm sure."

"We used to ignore that kid. Now you're telling me he's the Chosen One?"

"Shut up, Carl."

"I'm just saying --"

"Hey, look over here! Oh! He looked at me!"

"He's intelligent!?"

"Well, duh!"

"But is he The One?"

"We should ask him."

"You can't just ask The One if he's The One!"

"He won't know if he's The One, that would prove he's The One."

"I'm confused…"

"Yeah, that makes no sense…"

"Carl's touching me!"

"Knock it off, Carl!"

They murmured and argued this way amongst themselves till Hoof spoke again. "I… I'm so happy, I… I haven't seen you in so long…" he said. His resentment had faded to wonder, and a tear of joy ran unbidden down his cheek. "I don't know what else to say. It's been so lonesome…"

"Yes, Hoof…" the Shadow People said, in one gentle, unified voice. "We understand. "

"We've missed you, too, youngling…" said one of the voices.

"Youngling?" said another.

"Shut up, Carl!"

"But I, I sent you away," said Hoof, shame flowing into his cheeks. "I'm so sorry."

"We forgive you, Hoof. We're here now, that's what matters." Hoof smiled and the body of shadows pulsed. A moment passed. One of the beings cleared his throat. "So, anyway…"

Another moment passed. And another. And finally a shadow at the back muttered. "Well, this is awkward."

"Yeah, can we move this ahead a bit?" muttered another one as they began talking amongst themselves. "See, this is what I hate about being a collective."

"Exactly, nobody's in charge so nothing gets done."

"Carl keeps sliding up on me!"

"You like it."

"Knock it off, you two!"

"Someone ask him, please!"

"Yeah, ask him the thing."

"The thing?" asked Hoof.

"Er, yes, uh…" said one of the voices, glowing a little brighter and growing in size. "Our apologies, Hoof, but my colleagues are right, time is of the essence. In short, we are The *Dolämanu*, and we are… well, *travellers* is the closest word in your language. We live out our lives in the pathways of The Collectiverse between dimensions, inside the physical barriers of your world and all others. As a child, you were found to be one of only 83 beings across 8 known dimensions that was aware in any way of our existence, but till now the only one one of those beings with whom we have ever been able to communicate directly with.

"Under normal circumstances this would be a cause for celebration, but alas, our lives, our very existence as a species, is threatened by terrible forces beyond our control. We have taken great risk to find you again, for we believe… we hope… that you are the Chosen One, the being from our legends who might hold the key to saving our very species from extinction… but only if you willingly want to save us."

"Of course," said Hoof, who, like most of us with egos on this planet, knew that he had been born for a higher purpose. "What can I do? Anything!"

"Thank you, Hoof… but quickly! We grow weaker, and our psychic link with you may be lost…" said the Shadow People, already beginning to fade from his sight, their voices now becoming harder for Hoof to hear. "Our mission to you must not fail… do you agree to help us? Are you The One?"

"Yes, sure! I'm The One… I'm the One! What can I do? Name it!" said Hoof.

"Lean closer to us and we will transmit our instructions! Quickly! We haven't much time!"

Hoof put his ear up against the wall. He could feel the collected mass of the *Dolämanu* on the other side, and the Shadow

Person known as Carl whispered through the wall into Hoof's ear. Hoof considered what he'd heard, and nodded gravely. "I'll do it."

"It is the only way…!" cried the *Dolämanu* as a group, as every one of them began to fade from sight. "You must not … fail…!"

"Wait!" cried Hoof. "Will I see you again?" But the only response was silence. Hoof's resolve was fixed. He would not fail them, and he bravely did as he had been told. And on the security monitors downstairs, the concierge watched in disbelief as the guy in the gym who'd been talking to himself for the last ten minutes dropped his pants and took a standing dump on the gym floor. The police arrived ten minutes later.

The *Dolämanu* (which actually translates more closely to *frat pledges*) had taken a huge gamble, but it had paid off immensely. The task of fooling a less evolved species into public humiliation was frowned upon, but behind closed doors, the upperclassmen of Omega Omega Omega Spaxs were all in agreement, and every one of the new pledges who'd cosmically catfished Hoof had passed initiation. A statue of Hoof was commissioned and placed in their Secret Hall Of Idiots, right next to the one of Planjar Flazms, the poor Nebulon who had infamously been tricked into smoking his own procladoin in front of a Gloophum.

Malrong's Painting

After breakfast, Malrong resumed painting his apartment. This was the same thing he'd done for the last twenty-nine days. It dawned on him today that it seemed a little odd to take twenty-nine days to paint a one-bedroom apartment, and yet be no closer to finishing than when he'd started. Still, he was a pensioner with little to do, and happy for the diversion and the regular schedule.

What Malrong didn't know was that every night, for the past twenty-eight nights, a crew of troll contractors were dropping by to silently inspect his work. Invariably, they repeatedly and silently agreed that his work was not up to code, and would have to be redone. They would then silently replace every wall of his apartment with a new, unpainted wall and silently go back to where they had silently come from.

And that's just what was silently going to happen to Malrong again tonight. But that's modern Finland for you. Too many regulations, and too many union trolls making life worse for the little man.

El Puebla

"Excuse me, *jefe*?" asked the boorish patron, pronouncing the word *jefe* as jeff-ay. "Have you any authentic Cinco De Mayo dishes? I'm a rich, important so-and-so and I'm exceedingly tired of inauthenticity."

"*Amigos!*" yelled the waiter, clapping his hands. "*El Puebla!*"

Everyone in the dining room erupted in applause as a mariachi band rushed to the table in a flurry of stomping feet and clapping hands. As they yipped and sang, a three-foot high burrito was hurriedly delivered to the table by a trinity of altar boys, accompanied by a Catholic priest who prayed aloud in latin as he sprayed the dish with holy water from an aspergillum. The entire assemblage then broke into a spirited flamenco, and they all danced back into the kitchen from whence they'd appeared.

Everyone then fell into a breathless hush.

The patron eyed the dish with suspicion. "A large burrito? I could get something like this in any Latin quarter in any city in the world. I asked for something authen –"

He was interrupted by tiny gunshots and explosions from within the burrito. A tiny flag reading "1862" burst out. The patron's monocle fell from his surprised face and into his bowl of guacamole as a stampede of British bangers, emerald-green Spanish flies, and rivulets of Dijon mustard burst from within the folds of the burrito, frantically attempting to fortify and occupy various strategic locations around the table.

All the while, from deep within the burrito came a deep, trembling and growing rumble, rising in volume. When it could rise no longer, the inner folds of the burrito burst open in a series of saucy, convulsive spasms. A wildly hooping and hollering herd of patriotic tamales riding chiles burst out. Within moments the tamales had routed the occupiers, chasing them back into the burrito from whence they had emerged. The burrito grew in size again, spasms rocking its surface, until it exploded in a steaming hot spray of sauce and cheese.

As the smoke cleared, the burrito lay in shreds, spent by the tiny micro-war. The boorish patron, covered in juices, was speechless. The onlookers clapped their hands in adulation as a chorus of "Bravo! Oh, I say, bravo! Outstanding presentation!" washed over the kitchen staff, who were now leaning in from the kitchen door, taking proud stage bows.

"More mescal, *señor*?" asked the waiter, pouring another large portion, knowing full well that, for a boorish patron, nothing underlined local authenticity like reality-breaking insobriety. "Yes," replied the boorish patron, who'd already decided he would leave no gratuity. "And leave the bottle."

Fish Night Jamboree, 1973

In the early evening of July 12, 1973, the ever-darkening sky had finally cracked open as it dropped what would be the heaviest summer deluge any of the regulars at *Hullabaloo's Family RV & Campsite* could recall. But even the rain could not dampen the cheer and good times going on, and for good reason.

Rain or shine, Thursday nights were always "Fish Night Jamboree" in the huge festival mess tent in the centre of the campground, conveniently located just off exit 76 on Highway 101. Fish were on the fry and corn was on the boil, and all other manner of sea-food adjacent goodness was streaming steadily into the mouths of happy campers listening to the Hallaballeers Jug Band as they murdered that nights' setlist of ballads, folk tunes and country songs. Truth be told they only knew about thirty songs; and none of them very well, but they were halfway through their second set when the stranger appeared.

He was dripping from head to toe, and his skin was soaked right through to the skin. Though some would later recount that his soggy, drooping sou-wester was made of fire, that is of course an exaggeration. It was actually made of normal sou'wester material, but his galoshes were so waterlogged he might as well have been wearing buckets for shoes, and some swear that he was.

A few people who were close to the door made a fuss over how wet he was. They asked him if he wouldn't like to take off that jacket and dry off near the potbelly stove, but he made little to no response. Gretel Henderson claims she actually brought him a bowl of chowder to warm his bones, but that he refused to take it, much less even acknowledge that she was talking to him. He just kept watching the band with detached eyes as black as coal. The camp ground sure did take all kinds, she thought, but after a while, like everyone else, she paid the stranger no mind.

But halfway through the the band's third criminally rendered cover of 'Bad Moon Rising', a low wailing moan rose above the din, growing in volume till even the musicians themselves stopped to gape at the stranger standing by the entrance.

He seemed to have grown by at least four feet, and his hands were outstretched towards the terrified kitchen staff who were watching over the boil pots and frying pans. "Beware," he moaned again, some swearing at this point his head had become swollen with rage, and that they could see gills on either side of his throat. "Beware all ye who cook the flesh of the fishies!" Then he turned his baleful glare on the campers. "Beware all ye who eat the flesh of the fishies! Beware ye the punishing fins of the land trout, lest it consume ye!"

And then a huge rip appeared in the roof of the tent and a thunderous great trout, forty feet long if it was three, crashed through and flopped towards the stranger. People screamed as he took out a harpoon gun from under his peacoat, hollering "Do yer worst!"

As the huge thrashing fish landed on the stranger the tent collapsed. The crowd became a mad scramble of extremities fighting for exits, running to cower in their tents and camper vans. Some people immediately jammed their keys into the ignition and raced out to the highway, septic and electrical hookups be damned, never to return to Hullabaloo's again. Of the campers who stayed put, it wasn't till dawn that any of them dared venture outside and check in on the damage to the ruined and smouldering mess tent.

No trace was ever found of either the stranger, nor any great vengeful hell trout. Authorities chalked it up to mass hallucination, brought on by undercooked clams.

But that's what the Fish Cops always want you to think.

Nondescript

A nondescript man entered a nondescript convenience store where, amidst nondescript aisles, he found a nondescript bag of chips on a nondescript shelf.

There was no nutritional information, bar code, ingredients or expiry date on the bag; just the words "Bottomless Chips" on the front in a bold but nondescript font. He offered a nondescript amount of money to the nondescript cashier who mumbled: "Meh."

The nondescript man opened the nondescript bag of chips.

Instantly, swarms of extremely descript hands, paws and talons erupted from the bag. They clawed and punched and pulled at his face, and hauled him inside the bag as he uttered a nondescript sound. The nondescript bag resealed itself in mid-air and fell to the ground in a nondescript fashion.

The nondescript cashier picked up the nondescript bag with a pair of nondescript tongs and returned it to its nondescript shelf, and closed the nondescript store for the day. No sense staying open, it would just lead to another nondescript disappearance, because if one thing was true, the nondescript bag of chips could never have just one.

Singe of The Father

From the stern of *The Waffling Matilda*, Horagio Noerth smiled.

He closed his eyes and turned his face towards the mid-morning sun, basking in the glow as he took a deep breath of the ocean breeze. He'd lived no further than an hour from the Pacific Ocean for years, but had never spent any time in it, let alone even to the beach alongside it. But today was very different, because he was finally breaking one of many promises he'd made long ago to his father.

"Don't you go scuba diving!" his dad had once said. The old man didn't often get physical, but on that day he'd grabbed Horagio by the shoulders and shaken him hard. "Everrrrr!"

"Wetsuit?" asked his diving instructor, going through the first item on their safety checklist, and pulling Horagio to the present moment.

"Check!" replied Horagio.

He knew certain phobias could be passed on genetically, but over the years Horagio had realized that his struggles with aquaphobia were more a factor of his upbringing than anything else. Horagio's mom had died the year Horagio had turned thirteen, and while his dad had once admitted he was sad about it, the old man seemed content to live in denial of anything more, and the emotional distance between them had only grown with the passing of time. Facing his fears or his emotions had never been his dad's thing, and Horagio was ashamed of him for it.

"Flippers?"

"Check!"

"You sleeping?" his dad would sometimes ask, sitting on the edge of Horagio's bed in the middle of the night. His eyes were either wide-open and bloodshot, or tightened crows-feet slits, depending on his drug or drink of choice at the time. "I couldn't sleep," he'd say, though it was anybody's guess if he'd even tried. "You know, my dad didn't love me. My mother said he just wasn't the same after he got back from the war. But he didn't love her, either. Not really. I guess he couldn't. She shouldn't have married him. They shouldn't have had me. But you're lucky your dad loves you." And then he'd cry himself to sleep on the foot of the bed, leaving his son wide awake with more questions than answers.

"Oxygen tank?"

"Check!"

Sometimes his dad would say "The Nazis captured your grandad's whole squad and did experiments on them." Or sometimes it was along the lines of "he got some really weird tropical disease at Okinawa" or "he smoked some bad reefer when they were liberating the Netherlands" or the problematic "he picked something up from those French girls on furlough…"

"Ballast belt?"

"Check!"

"It's tough to explain, son," his dad would say. "You know how most people are made of water... well, whatever happened to your granddad in that lab in Antarctica? Well, it messed with his DNA and he passed it on to me, and I passed it on to you. Look, it's science, just be careful around water, okay? Be careful around water!"

"Face mask?"

"Check."

The on-again, off-again rules around water in the house were contradictory at best. Sometimes you could drink it, but only through a straw, to make sure it didn't touch any external part of your body. At one point they could drink water by letting ice-cubes melt in their mouths. Other times, you could only drink it if your body produced it, so sweat, blood, tears and pee was fine, although Horagio had never let himself get thirsty enough to try the latter. Taking a bath or a shower was a non-starter. They'd exfoliate with dry loofahs or scrub brushes, and only use dry shampoo or bathing oils (never mind that they were water-based, as Horoagio never bothered to point out). They had everything dry-cleaned, which was expensive, so they went without in other areas. Dirty dishes piled up undone till Horagio finally managed to convince his dad to get them a second-hand dishwasher.

"Cheaper than buying a new house, right?" his dad had joked.

"Depth gauge?"

"Check!"

Over the years the rules would change, evolve and rotate. Booze wasn't water, of course, according to the rationale, so that kept dad happy as a pickle, most of the time. If their dehydration got bad his dad would score saline from a medical sales rep he knew, and they'd hydrate intravenously. Horagio tried many times to reason with his dad, but there was no negotiating with him. He tried to rebel when his father wasn't looking, but invariably the old man would catch him about to break whatever cardinal rule was in place, and it would only strain their relationship further.

"Regulator?"

"Check!"

The old man had been hitting the bottle hard the day Horagio had told him he was going to get therapy. "Don't go see a shrink! They won't believe you! You think I'm lying?!" The man's mind was clearly unraveling under the weight of his fear, and Horagio had had enough. After screaming at each other for an hour, they both sat down at the kitchen table, and his dad poured him his first shot of whiskey. "There's no easy way to tell you this son," he said. "But if you're old enough to share a drink with me then I guess you're old enough to know the truth."

"Dolphins!"

"What?" asked Horagio. He gazed out to where his instructor was pointing; a flash of fins and bottle-noses breached the waves, clicking and chirping no more than a few boat lengths off the stern.

"We're sodium mutants, son," his dad had told him that day. "Our external skins are covered in an invisible sheet of it. So you go do your touchy-feely shit, but it's not gonna change anything! Therapy's not gonna help you. Fuck it, you might as well go scuba diving, then!" his old man had laughed, but Horagio had seen the look in his eyes. His father was afraid of water. And he was no longer going to live with his father's fear.

"Should we wait til the dolphins have moved away?" asked Horagio.

"No way, man!" his instructor replied. "This is a sign, you're goin' in with those guys! They're waitin', dude!"

"Fine," the old man had said, coldly. "You're a big man now? You know everything, big shot? You go ahead, you take those scuba lessons. See if I care. But just so you know, sodium's a soft, highly reactive metal, and when it comes into contact with water, it readily and violently loses its outermost electron to form cations with a plus one charge. That produces hydrogen gas, and it doesn't play nice with sodium. It's science, buddy." And with that, his dad had left the room, and had never uttered a single word to him again. That was over a year ago.

Horagio flopped over to the starboard and took a deep breath. He put the respirator in his mouth, checking one last time to be sure it was functioning. His instructor gave him the thumbs up. He counted to three, and dropped backwards over the gunwale. As he touched the water, he exploded violently, frightening off the dolphins and blowing a huge hole in the side of the boat. The crew frantically began to bail, and the captain radioed for the coast guard.

Sitting on a deck chair in the cockpit, bundled up in blankets like a homeless person and holding a bottle of rum in a paper bag, Horagio's father laughed, long and hard. "Science!" he snarled, and took a huge swig.

Park Bench

man walking through the park one day sat down on a wooden bench.

"The hell is this?!" said the bench. Of course, the man didn't answer, exactly as the bench knew he wouldn't, for the bench had long grown accustomed to being ignored, since no-one can hear the inner thoughts of a park bench.

"Oh, no, please don't introduce yourself first!" glowered the bench. "I'm just a bench, right? Who cares what I think about being sat on, huh?"

The man said nothing.

"I wasn't always a bench, you know!"

The man said nothing.

"I said I wasn't always a bench, you know!" said the bench again. "I was a tree once! Way older and taller than you! What are you like, sixty, seventy? Five foot ten? Ha! I was a ninety foot tall, ninety year old tree! I outlived every other seed in my bud, I did! Squirrels got some of 'em. The wind blew some of 'em into farmers fields and they got choked out. But not me. I found purchase in the soil, and I grew! I was the tallest tree for miles around!"

The man said nothing.

"Then what happened, you ask?"

The man was not asking this at all.

"I'm glad you asked. Then I got chopped down! And let me tell you one thing, old man – when a tree falls in the forest, all the other trees hear it! Sounds like this!" The bench then screamed for a solid eight minutes without interruption. "What do you think of that?" he asked when he thought he'd made his point.

The old man didn't think of it at all.

"Do you hear me?"

No, he certainly hadn't.

"There ain't no screams like mycelial screams cause mycelial screams don't stop!" rapped the tree, stopping then just the same, to see if the old man would say anything.

The old man said nothing.

"Then I got taken to a lumber mill. A lumber mill! Any idea what that's like? You think the buzz saws are the loudest thing you'd hear in a lumber mill? No. It's trees screaming! Like this!" And the tree screamed again for another very long couple of minutes to illustrate.

The man said nothing.

"That's the sound we all made when we were sawed into boards and planks and two-by-fours and bundled into piles and thrown into a dry kiln." And the tree illustrated this part of his journey approximating those sound effects as best he could, which was not very well.

"Then most of me got stacked in the lumber yard!" he said, making stacking sounds. "Then some of me got separated from the rest of me and piled onto the back of some guy's truck!" Driving truck sounds. "Then what was left of me was cut into same-size pieces and sanded down!" Sanding sounds, punctuated by screaming. "Then all those pieces of me got assembled through these metal slats and drilled and bolted into place!" Mouth sounds and screams. "Then I realized I'm a bench in some public park in some city somewhere!" Scream. "People sit on me!" Scream. "Eat on me!" Scream. "Sleep on me!" Scream. "Carve their initials into me!" Scream.

The man said nothing, continuously, for nearly forty minutes, as the bench went on, punctuating every iteration, milestone or trial of his long bench life with screams and bad foley. It had gone through such hardships such as the changing of seasons, dry rot, repainting, being set on fire by kids, wood stain, skateboard punks, and was just getting around to name every breed of dog that had urinated on it when the old man stood up.

"Oh, you're leaving now?" griped the bench.

The old man said nothing.

"Fine. But next time you even think of sitting on one of us benches —" The old man grasped his heart and fell back down on the bench. "What's wrong?" asked the tree, concerned. "Whoa, hey, old guy! You okay? You having a heart attack?"

The old man said nothing, because the old man had died, but only the bench heard him fall. The bench screamed for help as the sun went down, but it wasn't until the next morning when a jogger noticed the old man and called the paramedics. The bench added 'trapped under a dead man for nine hours' to the long list of indecencies it had endured.

The Presumption of Grant Portflange

"I hope I'm not being presumptuous," said Grant Portflange, seated at a table on a small raised platform at the head of the crowded outdoor patio of *Chez Toi Bistro*. "But I believe I have your undivided attention!"

He removed his top hat and monocle before standing, and if there had been any doubt before, he was definitely now the centre of attention, as those had in fact been the only articles of clothing he'd been wearing in the first place.

As if on cue, the jazz trio to his left dropped into a smooth walking bass number. Grant smiled and began to sing.

> "Please let me address
> my state of undress,
> that I must confess,
> has been caused by duress,
> which I will now redress.
> But let me digress:
> Take it, boys!"

The drummer did a moderately awkward solo fill, then the band vamped for a few bars as a waiter brought Grant a covered serving tray, placing it on the table in front of him before retreating back into the restaurant.

"My name is Grant Portflange, and I'm going tell you how I won the world, but lost my soul. And I'm going to begin," he said, lifting up the silver plate cover, revealing several pounds of raw liver. "... by turning this plate of meat into an excellent pâté."

He clasped his hands to his sides and knelt very low to the ground, then he bellowed and leapt into the air like a breaching whale. He landed hard and began to writhe and undulate on the plate of liver, moaning and grunting all the while.

Some people gasped. Others giggled and took photos. Some averted their eyes and others left their seats in disgust, but not the sour-looking man in the third row. He'd been holding a notepad up to that point, his pen hovering above the paper in anticipation of the scathing comments he would will through it. But instead, his furrowed eyebrows relaxed. He closed his book, sheathed his pen and leaned back in his seat as a smile cracked his face open for the first time in years.

"Finally," thought Jamp Knoshblatt, the notoriously pessimistic entertainment reviewer of *Meat Poets Magazine.* "Someone's been listening."

Garl Swerves

"**S**hit!" yelled Garl as he swerved hard left to avoid the Boeing Airbus that had come out of nowhere. His car began to fishtail. His wife, Ladle, began to scream and clutch the seat, holding on for dear life. "I told you not to cut through the airport!" she wailed, and who could blame her? Garl looked in the rearview mirror. There wasn't much time left; the pygmy rhino in his backseat had already started giving birth to mewling plaid kittens.

"Watch out!" screamed Ladle, pointing at the group of nuns jaywalking directly in their path. Garl swerved hard right to avoid the nuns.

"You and your shortcuts!" hollered Ladle. "*Yes, me and my shortcuts,*" thought Garl as he swerved left again to avoid the tricycling Cthulhu. "*Marriage. What bliss,*" he thought. "*She always wants to be on time, but she's never ready when we need to leave.*"

He very narrowly missed the family of low-flying paragliding yeti but only because they dispersed to let him pass. He heaved a quick sigh of relief but he should have been paying more attention, because one second later they had run straight into an *Equal Rights For Ghosts* protest march.

Garl grimaced as a dozen or more angry ghosts shook their incorporeal fists and hurled curses at him as they phased through his car. "Asshole!" "Fuck the living!" "Boo!" "Sorry! Sorry," he said through gritted teeth.

"What is wrong with you?!" screamed Ladle as she tried to hide her face in embarrassment, flinching despite herself as ghosts gibbered and passed through the cabin of the car with no damage to themselves, the passengers or the contents of the car.

"Oh, relax, they're ghosts. Nobody got hurt!" snapped Carl, his eyes rolling. "What about our feeeelings…?" yelled one ghost who happened to hear his phantophobic comment as they cleared the last of the protesters.

Garl expertly avoided the next several unexpected obstacles in their path, but as with all things, there was an end to his run of good luck and he, Ladle and the plaid Rhino kittens (and mother) all careened right into a worm-hole that opened up in their path and swallowed them whole.

***

Eight weeks later, Garl's car came bursting out of a gigantic cake at a party in Las Vegas. Frosting and vanilla innards sprayed as Garl's car swerved hard right to avoid the assembled party guests, hard left through the window, hard right through the parking lot and into several lanes of oncoming traffic. This necessitated a series of multiple left and right swerves, then a hard u-turn back across the other lanes of oncoming traffic from the other direction, and finally a hard swerve straight up until they finally came to a slow, teetering stop atop the neon sign outside the *Leaning Tower of Pizza.*

"Finally," muttered Ladle from the passenger seat as he turned on the wipers to clear the windshield of icing. She looked at her watch. "And we're late. You're the worst driver. I should leave you."

"Don't threaten me with a good time," retorted Garl.

Annoyed, she rolled down the passenger side window and leaned out. She could see the dazed party guests through the shattered window of the party room, picking themselves up, clearing and wiping frosting and filling out of their hair, ears and other orifices. "Aw, dammit."

"What?" said Garl.

"Dammit!" repeated Ladle, slouching into a pout in her seat.

"What?"

"I knew we should have left earlier. We need to go back."

"Why?"

"Someone else got them plaid rhino kittens."

Hunnerds Of Cullers

It was a Monday in mid-October in 1963, and little Shanka Norplank smiled darkly as she pulled her little red wagon to school, her mouth set in a determined clench. The eyes behind her taped up horn-rimmed glasses were narrowed to dark slits, and her brain snickered "heh-heh-heh" on an endless loop. It would still be a full twelve years before she joined a cult, but this was her first mantra.

On the little red wagon sat a rough cardboard box, about two feet high. It had been crudely coloured in orange and green paint to resemble a giant Crayola crayons box; a red arrow with white uppercase lettering indicated the presence of a BILT-IN-SHARPNER around the back, and greenish lettering on the orange cover promised HUNNERDS OF CULLERS inside. Shanka had spent all weekend finishing this project, and she was very proud of herself.

The idea for this box had come to Shanka last Monday, when Djuniper Czlarng had come to "Show and Tell" with the latest sensation: a giant, brand new box of 64 Crayola crayons. Djuniper wasn't about to share her new crayons - they were brand new, after all - but she had agreed to let every kid in class sharpen one of their own crayons with the built-in sharpener at the back of the box. That waft of waxy, new crayon smell had intoxicated Shanka. But Shanka didn't have any crayolas, and nobody would lend her one of theirs. She was stricken with loss.

The resentment and sorrow ate away at Shanka for the rest of the morning, and when she snuck back into class during lunchtime and tried to sharpen one of Djuniper's crayons when no-one was there, she'd been caught red-handed by Djuniper herself. They had struggled, and Djuniper had poked Shanka in the eye with 'raw umber', crayon #665233.

When Shanka told the teacher, it was Shanka herself who'd been scolded for touching things that didn't belong to her, and - insult to injury - she'd been sent home with a reprimanding note for her parents to sign. Well, she was going to have the last laugh.

The bell was ringing just as Shanka entered the schoolyard. She grunted as she lifted the heavy box carefully off the wagon, struggling to carry it up one, two, three, four concrete steps and through the open door of the red brick schoolhouse. She stashed the box under her jacket in her cubby at the back of the classroom, and she was slick with sweat and panting as a sly, devilish grin settled on her face.

It was her turn for show-and-tell today, and at ten-thirty she was going to bring this huge box out to the front of the class. All the kids would be so jealous, and they'd all want to see it. And when she'd finished her speech and they all raised their hands, she was going to pick Djuniper to use the sharpener first. Any colour she'd like. And if she'd timed it right, the quaaludes would be wearing off on the badger inside the box by then.

The Original Meerkat

As he trudged home for lunch, Flench Dearn kept his sad head down, the perfect picture of insecurity, misery and self-loathing. Was he the good, decent person he wanted to be, or was he the so-called 'self-centred knob' Leslie had just broken up with? He had a lot of ambition and at least a modicum of talent, and while he didn't resent the success of his peers, his own television writing career had failed to launch, his personal life was in shambles yet again, and all he could wonder was why.

As he approached the long-abandoned, dilapidated building on the corner at Broadview and Danforth, a peripheral flicker caught his eye.

He could have sworn just yesterday the whole storefront had been covered in concert posters and photocopied tear-away sheets hawking everything from rooms for rent to guitar lessons to drug trial testing. But those were all gone, and beneath the tape marks and glue residue still covering every inch of glass, an old neon sign feebly buzzed an invitation out to the world through the dust and grime.

Open

With the posted bills gone he could make out the remnants of elegant painted lettering on the glass that extolled this establishment's virtues: *Cheap Eats. Quick Service. No Diner is Finer. No Cobras. No Hawks. No Credit. No Questions.*

Looking up above the door, Flench noticed a worn and weathered ornamental metal sign swinging gently in the breeze. Upon it was a logo and stylishly intricate art deco lettering that read: *The Original Meerkat, Est. 1924.*

Open

He knew he'd definitely never noticed the sign before. Could he be that oblivious, he wondered, hating to admit that he was, and he spiralled back into melancholy. As he hung his head and turned to shlep home, he thought "... and do what? Another lonesome lunch? Another pity-party of one?"

Open

He lifted his head, took a deep breath, and walked up to the wood and glass double doors. He reached for the ornate brass handle, and as the thumb latch fell with a deep, echoing click, time seemed to slow down. Black spots danced in his eyes and he became light-headed and slightly nauseous; somehow his hand could not let go and he was dragged off his feet as the door swung inwards with a cloying whisper. The doorknob let his hand go and he fell flat on his face on the hardwood floor as the door swung shut behind him.

Flench looked up. He no longer felt dizzy, and although his eyes took a moment to adjust to the dim interior, his ears distinctly heard Elvis, both far away and far too close, drifting down around him like smoke. "I forrrgot… to rememberrr… to forget herrrr…." came the half-speed lyrics, like a jukebox on downers that knew the lyrics by rote but was exhausted of hearing itself.

He stood up. The sunlight filtering in seemed muted and timid, unable or unwilling to reach very far through the dirty windows, but it seemed like he'd stumbled into some kind of deserted hole-in-the-wall lunch counter. It was a chrome, pastel and sepia-toned affair, deep and narrow with booths on the left and a formica-topped lunch counter with round, plush red leather stools on the right.

He had always been drawn to places like this. He didn't feel like he was an old soul, exactly, but rather... well, he'd never been able to figure out why he was both at home and uneasy in these sorts of places. Old places just made him feel... *present* was almost the right word, he supposed. Creaky but beautifully stained hardwood flooring. Faded but solid beadboard paneling. Metal signs for Coca Cola and Black Kat cigarettes. He grew so enraptured by the decor that it took a few moments before he finally registered the large meerkat staring at him.

It stood erect on a stool behind the counter, frozen in place with one paw on the handle of a manual coffee grinder. It wore a mustard-stained apron and a drab, olive-coloured garrison cap and its unblinking, unflinching eyes were narrow, suspicious slits.

"Oh, hey, hi," blurted Flench in what he hoped was a calm, soothing voice. "I didn't see you there, buddy..."

An awkward moment passed before the meerkat's fixed gaze relaxed... barely. It slowly and deliberately resumed grinding as another smaller meerkat leaned out from behind it to get a better look at Flench. This one's eyes were comically huge, owing to the coke-bottle-thick horn-rimmed glasses behind which they sat, and it held a spatula in its paw. On the flat-top grill behind it, Flench noted a sizzling pile of what looked like corned beef hash.

As the meerkats continued to stare at him, Flench began to feel awkward. "I'll just let myself out," he stammered, stepping backwards slowly into the door. To his dismay, it did not budge. He whirled and fumbled with both hands to no avail; there was no handle or knob of any kind on this side of the door.

Through the grungy double door windows, he could see a young couple walking up, hand in hand, though far away as if he were looking through the wrong end of a telescope. "Hello!" yelled Flench, pounding on the doors. "Hey! I'm trapped in here! Can you open the door, please? Hey!" But if they could hear him, they gave no sign as they walked by and out of sight.

Flench turned back to the counter, ready to plead to be let out, but the words died in his throat. There were now countless pairs of curious meerkat eyes gazing at him from everywhere throughout the diner.

Meerkats peering from stools at the counter.

Meerkats peeking over the back of booths.

Meerkats gaping as they hung by their tails from the light fixtures.

Meerkats staring from inside the dispensary slots of the upright vintage soda vending machine.

Meerkats peeping from the pockets of the long abandoned, dusty peacoat jackets on the coat hooks along the wall beside him.

Each time he made eye contact with one, Flench flinched and gasped audibly, and each time it triggered an involuntary but beautifully synchronized recoil in every meerkat in the room. And though they shuddered as one, none of them retreated; instead they drew closer. Flench brought his hands up to his face, closed his eyes and waited for death. He hoped it happened quickly; that they were skilled killers, or had some kind of meerkat venom that would render him dead before he felt any pain as they devoured him.

But then he heard a quizzical chirp below and slightly to his left. Flench carefully peeked out between his fingers and looked down, till he met the gaze of a meerkat in a tuxedo jacket.

It purred reassuringly, then clapped its paws together and whistled. A busboy meerkat suddenly dropped from the ceiling, whipping the stool clear of crumbs and dust with several smart cracks of his bar towel before scurrying away. The tuxedoed meerkat gestured for Flench to sit, which he did.

The coffee station meerkat plopped a steaming cup of joe down in front of him. The spectacled meerkat at the grill slapped together a plate of piping hot breakfast mash and slid it down the counter to him. Then all three meerkats paused, staring at him expectantly. Then down at the plate. Then back at him.

"Um," Flench gulped. "I'm not really… hungry…" Every meerkat in the room hissed and took one step closer. "O-okay, okay," he stammered. "I'm sorry! I'll try!" He brought a nervous and quivering forkful of corned beef hash up to his mouth.

He looked around.

Every meerkat eye in the room was on him.

He opened his mouth. Every meerkat in the room seemed to stand even taller now; even the jukebox ground to a groggy, vertiginous and pregnant halt.

Flench took the food in his mouth. It was warm on his tongue. And… savoury. Familiar, somehow. And comforting. He slowly put the fork down and chewed carefully. Colour came back to his cheeks. The tip of his nose buzzed with warmth. Every chew of every morsel seemed to release a sense of calm that washed over him in waves, and he swallowed.

Every meerkat in the room leaned in ever closer towards him.

"Oh, my God," said Flench.

Every meerkat eye in the room widened.

"This is the best corned beef hash I've ever had," Flench said at last, and it was true.

Flench looked up at the coffee station meerkat. Coffee arched a slightly miffed-looking eyebrow, glancing down to the steaming coffee mug and back up at Flench. Flench took a tentative sip, swishing the dark brown liquid around in his mouth, letting it wash over his tongue and teeth before he swallowed. As the notes and aftertaste hit their marks on his palette, Flench's body tensed. His eyes rolled back and took his head with them, and he had an involuntary dry orgasm. "It's so good," he wept as the last contraction left him. "I never knew it could be so good…"

Many chirps of meerkat joy and relief washed over the diner. The feeling in the room was absolutely electric as Tuxedo held his left paw straight up in the air and whistled to the entire colony.

Every meerkat stood at attention, and when Tuxedo brought his paw down, they rushed into the kitchen, grabbing aprons and tiny cooks' hats, scrubbing their paws at the sink and forming prep lines at every station. And then they went to work.

For the next several hours, Flench was treated to a taste-test smorgasbord of all-day breakfast splendour. Each dish was more elaborate and better than the last. Perfectly seasoned plates of eggs in many styles. Savoury rashers of bacon, glistening and perfectly cooked. Thick, butter-oozing pancakes with maple syrup that tasted like it had come out of the tree yesterday. Stuffed crêpes with textures that made his pupils dilate, and an almond croissant that melted so amorously on his tongue that for a moment Flench believed he understood heroin.

Each elegantly presented dish was brought to him, and whisked away as soon as he thought he couldn't eat another thing. He would then be surprised at the ravenous appetite he found when his eyes fell upon the next expertly plated offering. Flench's mind was blown repeatedly; his exploding tastebuds made shrapnel.

As Coffee kept coffee flowing into his cup in a never ending stream, Flench relished in the proliferation of condiment choices; staples as plain and essential as ketchup and peanut butter, as spicy as sriracha or as exotic as sofritos or yuzu kosho. He was awash in a never-ending variety of compotes, marmalades, and spreads. He tasted all manner of root vegetables au gratin, and bowls of hearty grits and granolas. He sampled sides of fresh berries, smashed breakfast potatoes with rosemary, piping hot cornbread, and a life-affirming avocado toast that despite no longer being on trend was so delicious he vowed to murder anybody that offered him anything of lesser quality, anywhere, ever.

When it was evident to both Flench and his hosts that not a single morsel more could cross his lips, his place was cleared fastidiously and the check laid before him on a plate, along with mints and a toothpick. Flench looked at the slip of paper with some apprehension. Surely the feast he'd just experienced was going to come with a kingly sum attached. But how could he have said no, at any point?

He picked up the bill and there, written in a scribbled but refined hand the most comforting shade of Bic ballpoint blue was the ludicrous price:

$5

Surely this was a mistake, but then Flench remembered the

sign he'd read outside: *Cheap Eats*. He reached for his wallet. He counted all the bills and coins he had on him, which amounted to just shy of twenty-seven dollars. "Keep the change," he said, laying the cash down on the counter as a flurry of paws and tails whisked it away. "I only wish I had so much more to give you."

He looked up at Coffee, who was hard at work grinding more beans. "This was… your coffee was, I mean… thank you so much," he stammered. "I'll never forget it." Coffee gave him a perfunctory, world-weary nod. Mustard Stain Coke Bottle Eyes had already turned his back, dropping onions, potatoes and chopped meat on the grill, the beginnings of what was sure to be another stellar hash.

Flench watched quietly as activity went on around him, but where once he'd been the centre of attention, he now felt a bit out of place. "I'm… uh… I'm gonna go now," he said, not wanting to wear out his welcome but not entirely sure he was free to go.

He got up off the stool and took a tentative shuffle towards the door. "I'll be back, though," he said. Without looking up, Coffee gave him a back-handed wave. The front door now swung open, and Flench took that as his cue. But halfway out he turned back. "So… are you guys *really* just meerkats?" he asked.

All meerkat work stopped, and a hush fell on the room.

Coffee slowly turned to stare at Flench, his face a mask of disdain. Every other pair of meerkat eyes (and, in the case of the meerkat with the peg leg and eye-patch, her single one) fell sadly to their feet. Tuxedo began to whimper. Mustard Stain began to hiss and growl, till he could contain himself no longer and began striking the grill with his meat tenderizer.

Every meerkat in the diner began to howl, their voices joining into a harmonious and unsettling din as they rushed him. Startled, Flench recoiled and stumbled backwards, tripping over his feet and falling the rest of the way out of the diner and onto the sidewalk. He scrambled on all fours up against a fire hydrant, cringing as he shielded his face, waiting to be mauled.

But nothing happened.

He peeked out between his fingers, but the door was now shut behind him. Nothing had followed him out of the diner. He looked up to see dozens of angry meerkats pressed up against the glass of the storefront windows, glaring at him. Tuxedo knocked on the window for his attention, then pointed angrily at one specific line of art deco lettering Flench had read before going in:

No Questions

"No Questions?" he said incredulously, only realizing his second faux pas as dozens of meerkats hissed behind dozens of facepalms, except for Coffee, who just glared and flipped him the bird. Then every meerkat scurried back into the darkness, and the neon sign flickered and buzzed one last time.

Closed

Before Flench could even stand, a deep rumbling sound grew, and the ground began to shake. Pigeons nesting on the eves fluttered off, and insects and rodents began to scurry and scuttle out from the cracks spreading out on the sidewalk. The entire diner shook. Hydro cables sparked and snapped off the building and sputtered to the concrete as *The Original Meerkat* rose before his eyes, lifting itself off ground, foundation and all.

Several passersby walked in front of, behind or around Flench, avoiding him but failing, or refusing, to give any indication that they had even noticed the building as it ascended, slowly at first, then gathered speed as it rose up, up, up until it was no more than a speck. It finally disappeared from Flench's sight with a flash of light and a final sonic boom.

There was nothing but a gaping, vacant hole in the ground where the building had once stood.

Flench stood up slowly, confronted yet again with the knowledge that he would never fully understand Toronto. But an idea was hatching in his brain, and he hurried home. He wrote all night, and by lunch the next day, he had a ten page treatment for a darkly humourous anthology series called *Tales From The Original Meerkat.*

When he met with the head of development at the Canadian Broadcasting Corporation a few weeks later, they had some initial notes, of course. It was, after all, a bit high concept, and they weren't sold on the title, and Flench agreed that yes, of course, the protagonists need not be meerkats, and yes, of course, the series could be set in Newfoundland. He didn't think the meeting had gone very well, but within a few weeks, the executive got back to him. After looking at his second draft; they felt he'd be great to collaborate with, and as long as he was open to more notes as they went along, they wanted to option his concept.

Flench was over the moon. Compromise or not, the years of hard work and rejection had finally paid off. As his series was being developed, he became an avid brunch patron at diners all over the city. He chose both dives and bougie venues equally, looking for inspiration as much, if not more, than a great meal, but no grill in the city came anywhere close to the quality or variety of *The Original Meerkat* menu, and how could they?

Sixteen months passed, and in the time it took for a bland and featureless condo to be built in the hole in the corner lot at Broadview and Danforth, his series, now a family drama titled *Sons and Otters*, premiered on CBC Television to great critical acclaim.

It was nominated for several Canadian Screen Awards, including Best Writing, which it did not win. But Flench took this in stride, proud that the series did take home top honours for Best Ensemble and Best Costume Design. He had great plans to take the show in new directions, but as generations of television creatives in Canada have learned, awards do not a second season guarantee, and *Sons and Otters* was canceled.

Flench put on a brave public face, but he was devastated. He tried to console himself with the advice of friends in the industry who assured him that none of it was personal, that none of it really mattered. He pitched new ideas to every production company he could meet, but nothing was landing.

He took long walks in neighbourhoods around the city, looking for *The Original Meerkat*. Maybe if he got in there one more time, he thought, and he didn't ask questions, he'd get the answer he wanted, the how and why of it all. He'd ask people on the street where the best (or worst) local greasy spoon was, but none of their recommendations ever measured up. As weeks turned into months, the whole thing began to feel like it had just been a dream.

On one of his soul-searching strolls his phone buzzed. It was a text from a producer he'd become friends with, telling him there was an opening for writers on her celebrated satirical program *This Hour Always Somehow Manages To Feel Way Longer*, and that he should submit his writer's packet as soon as possible.

He sighed. His heart wasn't in it, but he began tapping out his reply, thanking her for thinking of him, and yes, he'd send something right away, and that's why he didn't notice a familiar neon flicker in the window of a dingy storefront to his right as he walked by.

Open

He didn't see the new and ornately painted slogans on the window and wonder what they meant.

Under New Management

He was never going to know he had missed his second chance, but in the grand scheme of things, none of that mattered, because life isn't personal.

Predators Welcome

Like all of us, Flench was a tiny speck of sentience on a beautiful blue ball spinning in an infinite universe, and as he put his phone back in his pocket, a small smile found its way to his face, because the moment was ripe with promise and potential, and isn't that kind of freedom just wonderful?

Questions Only

About the Author

A New Brunswicker of Acadian, Brayon and franglais extract, Marcel St. Pierre is an award-winning writer, actor, improvisor, comedian, and producer who now calls Toronto home. A founding member and former Artistic Director of *The Bad Dog Theatre Company*, he has appeared in film and television and onstage across North America with *The Second City National Touring Company*, the Canadian Comedy-Awarding winning *Monkey Toast* and more. Follow him on social media *@shortweird*